*When Ellen's
perfect life shatters,
she has . . .*

Nowhere to Turn

*Divorced by her husband.
Shunned by her church.
Forsaken by God?*

R H O N D A   G R A H A M

Pacific Press Publishing Association
Boise, Idaho
Oshawa, Ontario, Canada

Edited by Bonnie Widicker
Designed by Tim Larson
Cover by Lars Justinen
Typeset in 11/13 Century Schoolbook

Scripture quotations in this book are from the New King James
Version.

Library of Congress Cataloging-in-Publication Data:
Graham, Rhonda.
    Nowhere to turn / Rhonda Graham.
        · p.   cm.
    ISBN 0-8163-1128-5
    I. Title.
PS3557.R218N68   1993
813'.54—dc20   92-33210
                                                                      CIP

93 94 95 96 97 ● 5 4 3 2 1

*When Ellen's
perfect life shatters,
she has . . .*

Nowhere to Turn

Dedication

To David, forever

Contents

Chapter 1

"I want a divorce."

The words hung heavily between them. Somewhere behind her, Ellen could hear a tinny jukebox playing country music. A waitress ambled by, coffeepot in hand. Everything looked so normal, so usual.

"What?"

He said it again. "I want a divorce." His jaw trembled slightly, and he clenched it.

She slumped in the chair, feeling like all the air had been sucked out of the room. She could almost see the words hovering in front of her. She looked at the table with their plates of half-eaten food. A numbness crept over her body, and she felt cold and anesthetized.

"You're joking, right?" She tried to give him his favorite cute smile, but her numb lips wouldn't respond.

He looked away. "No."

Silence. The diner buzzed with the conversation of other people. Cooks yelled orders in the back. Ellen's arms felt too heavy to lift off the table. She shivered, but didn't reach for her sweater draped across the back of the chair. She tried to think, to find something to say, but her brain felt frozen too. His words kept echoing in her thoughts—"I want a divorce; I want a divorce."

"Why?" she whispered. She wanted to scream, yell, demand an explanation. To ask him why, after seventeen years of marriage, he could say that. Her voice wouldn't cooperate. She tried again. It still came out in a croak. "Why?"

He refused to meet her eyes. "I'm not happy," he muttered as he slid the saltshaker back and forth on the table.

"What do you mean, you're 'not happy'?" Ellen asked. She tried to think of the past few years. When had this started? Ten years ago? Fifteen? When Jeff was born?

A flash of anger. "I'm just not happy, OK? I want—no, I *need* to get away." His voice rose. Heads whirled their direction.

Ellen took a deep breath and deliberately lowered her voice. "You're not serious. What about the church? What about your job?" *What about us?* she wanted to ask. "What about Jeff?" she asked aloud.

"I don't know," he replied hoarsely. "I just can't live with you anymore."

Ellen suddenly wondered if it was all a bad dream. Frank, balding and slightly paunchy, looked as familiar as he always did. He still had the gentle, kind face of a pastor. The words didn't fit. Nobody threw away seventeen years— especially not a pastor. The jukebox switched songs. A love song started playing. Frank turned his face away from her, his chin quivering. Ellen reached out to take his hand, but he pulled it out of her grasp.

"Let's talk about this at home," she suggested. She wondered at her own self-control. She didn't feel angry or sad. She felt numb. Dead. And plastic inside.

He nodded, stood up, and threw a few bills on the table. Ellen grabbed her sweater off the back of the chair and followed him out of the diner. By the time they reached the car, he had composed himself.

"Could this be midlife crisis?" Ellen asked quietly.

He shook his head. "No, I think I finally know what I want."

He turned on the windshield wipers. Ellen watched them sweep back and forth, never quite able to keep ahead of the downpour.

How did I miss this? she wondered. *Why didn't I guess sooner?* She thought of his silence at home, the late evenings at church, the distance between them. *But that's normal*, she mentally argued. *We're both busy, we have a teenage son, the church takes all our time.* She looked at Frank's profile. His jaw was set again.

"How long have you been feeling this way?" she whispered.

He didn't look at her. "Years. Maybe forever."

"When are you leaving?" she asked quietly.

"Tonight." A short reply.

"Tonight?" Ellen gasped. "Where will you stay? What about prayer meeting?"

"It's none of your business," Frank answered curtly.

Ellen slumped against the car door. Panic rose, and she fought it back down. *This isn't real*, she thought. *This can't be happening.*

"Why can't we take some time to talk about it?" she asked.

"I've thought about it for too long already. I'm leaving. Just lay off, will you?" he snapped.

She stared at him, wide-eyed. The gentle, quiet man she thought she'd married had disappeared. An angry, surly monster took his place.

They stopped in front of the house. Frank backed the car into the garage and popped the trunk lid. Ellen's icy fingers fumbled at her seat-belt latch. Finally, very slowly, she undid the buckle. Frank stepped out of the driver's side and left her sitting in the car.

"I'll keep up on all the bills, of course," he said as she climbed out of the car.

She walked numbly into the house and sat on the bed,

watching him pack. As his closet emptied, her panic rose.

"What am I going to tell Jeff?" she asked.

"Tell him what you want," he muttered.

She felt a flash of anger. "You're the one in the wrong here. You tell Jeff."

He slammed the lid down on the suitcase. "Fine."

"Why?" she whispered. "You still haven't told me why."

Frank stopped packing and looked at her a second. His face crumbled. "I'm sorry, Ellen. I never meant to hurt you." He drew a ragged breath. "I just can't stay married to you."

I am not hearing this, Ellen thought wildly. *I am not hearing this. This isn't Frank. It's a bad dream.*

"What did I do?" she whispered, fighting tears.

"It's just not right anymore. I have to get out and find out where I belong. If I don't, I'll kill myself." He whispered the last few words with intensity. "I need to start over. Everything's been choking the life out of me—you, the church, everything. I'm starting over in a new life, a new job, and—"

"Is there someone else?" Ellen whispered.

He pretended not to hear her.

"Is there someone else?" she asked, this time louder. Frank kept moving clothes out of the closet. "Answer me!" she yelled.

He stopped packing and looked at the floor. "Does it matter?"

Ellen felt a wave a nausea. "Who is she?" she hissed through clenched teeth.

He hesitated. "Look, there's nobody," he said, not meeting her eyes.

"Liar," she spat at him. "Tell me the truth."

He looked at the wall. "Why do you want to know this?"

"Because I have a right to know," she shot back.

They stared at each other for a few seconds. The front door slammed, and footsteps came toward the bedroom.

"Mom? Dad?"

"It's Jeff," Ellen whispered.

"In here," Frank called.

Jeff walked into the room and slouched against the wall. "Can I stay over at Brandon's tonight?" he asked.

"No!" Ellen said sharply.

Jeff drew back, surprised. "Man, what's with you?"

Frank walked over and put a hand on his shoulder. "I think we need to talk."

Jeff looked at both of them suspiciously.

"Your mother and I have decided to live apart for a while," Frank said quietly.

Your mother and I? Ellen thought and stifled a hysterical laugh. *Since when do I have any control over this?* She looked at the sudden rigidness in Jeff's shoulders and longed to hug away his tension the way she did when he was a little boy.

"That's cool," he said, his eyes guarded and his back stiff. "May I stay over at Brandon's tonight?"

Ellen gasped, and Frank threw her a warning glance.

"Listen, Jeff, this has nothing to do with you. It's between your mother and me." He put his hand on Jeff's shoulder reassuringly.

Jeff shrugged out from his grasp. "So you're getting a divorce. So what? Happens all the time, right?" His voice broke, and he ran from the room. They heard the back screen door slam.

Ellen jumped off the bed to follow him.

"Don't," Frank said, stopping her. "Let him go."

She whirled around, furious. "Fine thing for you to say, you cheating, irresponsible jerk. Get out! I can handle this myself. Get the hell out of this house!"

Frank stared at her, stunned. She had never raised her voice at him in their marriage, much less swore at him. She watched his reaction with a grim sense of satisfaction. She tried to control her anger, but it coursed through her, unchecked. "Are you happy now?" she spat at him. "You have destroyed two lives now—mine and your son's. Are you happy?"

He grabbed the last suitcase and strode toward the garage, not speaking. She followed him, still furious.

"I will fight you for everything—the house, custody of Jeff, everything. Got it?"

He ignored her, slammed the trunk lid, and climbed into the driver's seat.

"I'll be back later for the rest of my things," he said shortly. He looked at her, and his eyes filled. "I'm sorry, Ellen, for everything."

Ellen felt her own eyes fill, her anger deflated. "Frank, don't you love me anymore?"

Silence. He looked down. "I don't know if I ever loved you."

Closing the door beside him, he drove out of the garage and down the street. Ellen watched his taillights blur and disappear as her tears overflowed.

"Why?" she screamed to an empty garage. No response.

"Why?" she whispered, sobbing.

The anger felt flat. She walked zombielike to the bedroom and collapsed on the bed. Memories of the past few days and years came back. She thought of breakfast that morning. She'd made pancakes. She and Frank had talked about their vacation plans. Or had Frank talked at all?

"He'll be back," she whispered.

Her crying subsided a little. The back door slammed again, and she sat up and straightened her skirt.

"Frank? Is that you?" she called out.

Jeff's bedroom door slammed in response, and his stereo began playing loudly. She sighed and got off the bed. The last thing they needed was the neighbors hearing such music coming out of a pastor's house. She walked to Jeff's bedroom door and knocked.

"Jeff?" she asked, knocking louder.

No response. "Jeff?" This time louder.

"Go away," he yelled. "Just leave me alone."

"Jeff, your stereo . . ."

He threw the door open, his blue eyes bloodshot and red-rimmed. "Why can't you just leave me alone?"

Ellen felt her tears rising again. "Jeff," she pleaded.

His eyes filled, and he slammed the door again. The stereo stopped abruptly. The phone started ringing, and Ellen walked back into the bedroom and answered it automatically.

"Hello?" she heard herself say quietly and professionally.

Where did you get this kind of control? she asked herself. Inside she could feel herself stretching tighter and tighter.

"Ellen? This is Marsha Thune. We're waiting for Frank to start prayer meeting. Has he left yet?"

Ellen looked at the clock and fought hysterical laughter. "I'm sorry, Marsha. Frank was called out on a pastoral emergency. You'd better go ahead without him."

A sigh. A long silence. "Well, all right." Marsha's voice sounded anything but all right.

"I'll tell him you called," Ellen told her warmly.

"Fine. Goodbye."

"Goodbye."

She hung up and stared at the family picture on the night stand. So Frank hadn't even bothered to tell the church. The coward! Looking at the picture, taken two years before, she tried to guess Frank's thoughts. He looked happy in the picture. *Maybe he didn't tell the church because he's planning on coming back*, she thought.

The thought soothed her. *That must be it*, she mentally

decided. *He'll be back in a few days, and we'll take a long vacation together—then maybe get some counseling.* She looked around the room they'd decorated together when they bought the house ten years before. She put all thoughts of Frank's anger out of her mind and tried to remember the good times.

"Everything will work out for the best. God will work everything out," she whispered to herself.

But as soon as she said it, she remembered Frank's face. And she remembered his words. Ellen wanted to cry, scream, do anything to let the pain out. But the constriction inside only tightened. She thought of Frank's evasive comments about another woman and felt nauseated.

"There's no one else," she told herself as she paced the room. The walls of their lovingly decorated bedroom seemed to press in on her. Almost running from the room, she stopped in front of Jeff's door and knocked softly.

"Jeff?"

He opened the door a crack.

"Do you want to talk about it?" she asked.

He looked down and shook his head.

"It's not permanent," she told him. Ellen longed to wrap her arms around him, but he didn't open the door any farther. And more than anything, she wanted to believe her own words.

He shrugged and refused to meet her eyes. "Can I go over to Brandon's tonight?" he asked again.

Ellen sighed, feeling helpless. "I guess."

"Great." He opened the door and walked down the hall, duffel bag in hand. "I'll be home for supper tomorrow."

"God will work it all out," Ellen called after him, helplessly. *He will, won't He?* she inwardly questioned.

Jeff laughed shortly. "Yeah. Right." He stopped and turned to her. "Do you really believe that?"

Ellen gasped. "Of course! And so should you!"

He gave her a long look. "Then you're less with it than I thought you were."

"That's enough, young man," Ellen snapped. "I'm still your mother, and you'll talk to me accordingly!"

His shoulders slumped, and he lowered his eyes. "Sorry. Can I go now?"

Ellen nodded, unable to respond. *What did he mean, "less with it"? Did he know something?* The front door closed quietly, and Ellen felt the emptiness of the house press in on her. She longed to call a friend.

"Don't do it," she said to herself. "Frank will be back soon. No one needs to know about this."

She changed into a nightgown and washed her face. She watched herself in the mirror. A young thirty-nine, she decided. Her short dark hair swung around her face in a sleek bob. And except for a few stubborn pounds on her hips, her figure still looked slim and girlish. She wondered, again, if Frank had another woman.

"Don't think about it," she told herself. "God will take care of it."

With determination, she climbed into bed, turned off the light, and tried to sleep.

Chapter 2

When Ellen woke, it was still dark. A car drove by on the street, its headlights momentarily lighting the ceiling. Ellen lay on her back, staring at the darkness. The house felt too quiet.

It took a few seconds. Then everything came crashing back. She rolled over and hugged Frank's pillow close to her. The numbness remained. A cold, shaking feeling accompanied it. She clutched the covers tighter to her and tried to get warm. The nausea she'd fought earlier now returned. This time she couldn't fight it. Throwing the covers back, she raced to the bathroom and was violently ill. She felt no better afterward.

Lying on the floor of the bathroom, she felt tears start. "Why, God?" she cried. "Why is this happening? Haven't I been a good wife? Haven't I done everything I was supposed to?"

The tears dried up. She longed to cry more—cry until the terrible cold numbness could be washed away. But the tears refused to come.

"What am I going to do?" she asked herself.

The cold tile felt clammy beneath her. She sat up slowly and thought about going back to bed. The shaking remained. The bathroom clock read 5:00 a.m. And Ellen knew she couldn't sleep anymore.

She stood and rinsed out her mouth in the sink, then looked at her reflection. Dark brown eyes. Her black hair—which usually looked glossy—now hung limply around her pale face. Her eyes looked dead. Shuddering, Ellen turned away from her reflection and stripped off her nightgown. Stepping into the shower, she tried to wash all the memories away. Even the hot water failed to rid her of the cold feeling inside.

"I have to get a job," Ellen muttered as she washed her face. "And a lawyer."

A lawyer. It seemed too final. What if things did work out? What if Frank changed his mind?

"I'll wait on the lawyer," she said as she stepped out of the shower and wrapped herself in her big terry-cloth robe. The sight of Frank's robe, hanging on the hook next to hers, brought the helpless feeling back.

"Maybe he's just going through something," Ellen reasoned as she dressed carefully in her most professional skirt and blouse. "Maybe he'll be back."

But mouthing hopeful words did not eliminate the bleak feeling. She finished dressing automatically and blow-dried her hair without thought. Digging through her drawers, she found some makeup for her pale face. It felt good to cream it on.

The morning paper waited for her on the front doorstep. She brought it in, forced herself to drink a glass of milk, and sat down with a pen and a pad of paper. She wrote "To Do" across the top of the page.

Number one. Find a job. Ellen nibbled on the back of the pen. In what area? She didn't feel competent in anything.

"Well, they'll have to hire me anyway," she said with a feeling of bravado.

Number two. Find a lawyer. Who? Where? Frank always took care of things like that. She considered calling a lawyer in Frank's congregation but decided against it.

"I'll check the phone book," she told herself.

Number three. Talk to Frank. Ellen looked at it a minute, then crossed it off the list. *If he wants to talk, he can contact me*, she thought.

The sun began streaming in through the kitchen windows. Ellen stopped writing and stared at the beauty. She realized suddenly that she hadn't seen a sunrise since Jeff had the chickenpox ten years before. She turned back to her list.

Number four. Get own bank accounts. She looked at the other items on the list and switched this to number one. An image of Frank paying bills at the kitchen table came to mind, but she pushed it quickly away.

"You have to take care of yourself," she said aloud. Picking up the paper, she turned to the employment section and began scanning the list for possible jobs. Every one of them seemed to want three to five years' experience. Ellen blinked back tears.

"I will do this," she told herself firmly. "I will take care of myself."

Summoning a strength she didn't know she had, Ellen started writing down the names and phone numbers of any possible job leads. She looked at the clock. Seven o'clock. Still an hour before she could call on them.

After rinsing her glass in the sink, she walked determinedly into Frank's study. He seemed to be in this room more than any other. She choked back tears as she remembered all the late nights they had worked on sermons together in this room.

"Be strong," Ellen told herself firmly.

In one impulsive motion, she swept all of Frank's papers and notes off the desk and into the trash can. It made her smile. Frank was always too picky about his things anyway. Taking a clean sheet of paper, she started her résumé. As she finished the pitifully small list of jobs, she choked back tears again.

"Who's going to hire me?" she asked aloud.

She wondered how she could explain fifteen years of being a mother, pastor's wife, and church secretary. Aha! Church secretary. Ellen quickly rolled the paper back into the typewriter and added that to the list.

When she returned to the kitchen, the clock read ten after eight. Ellen picked up the phone and started dialing the numbers on the list.

"I'm sorry, we want someone with more experience."

"Do you have computer skills?"

"We're sorry. We filled that job yesterday."

The list got shorter. Ellen began to feel more and more discouraged. Finally, the last two on her list granted her interview times for that afternoon.

Smiling, Ellen grabbed her purse and résumé and left the house. Driving first to the nearest grocery store, she stopped and made extra copies of her résumé. The action made her feel good. She pushed thoughts of Frank out of her mind every time they intruded.

She stopped at the bank next. In less than half an hour, she transferred half the checking and all the savings into accounts in her name. She felt a little guilty about taking all the savings, but she figured Frank deserved it. Ellen left the bank feeling strong and in charge of her life. Every time she noticed herself feeling afraid, she reminded herself that she was competent.

Her first interview was with a law firm. A young, smart-looking lawyer took her résumé and barely looked at it. Ellen thought he appeared bored.

"Let's see. You haven't held a paying job since . . . um . . . 1977?" His face was carefully controlled, but Ellen could sense the derision in his tone.

She sat up straight and told herself to keep calm. "That's when my son was born. But if you look at the résumé, you'll see I did secretarial work for my hus—for a church."

He raised one eyebrow, looked at her for a second, then looked back at the résumé. "Do you have computer skills?" he finally asked.

Ellen dreaded this question. "No, but I'll take classes or whatever I need to learn how."

He put the résumé on the desk and gave her a wide false smile. "Thank you for stopping by. We'll let you know."

Ellen shook his hand and walked briskly out of his office. *Little snot! Just because he's young and rich and male he thinks he can condescend to me.* She got on the elevator and mentally shook her fist at the law firm.

She stepped outside the building into a slight drizzle. Ellen looked up the street, hating the town. She'd always hated this town. Frank had told her to be patient. It was only a temporary position. They'd move in a year or two. But a year or two turned into sixteen. Now Ellen figured she'd never get out of Riverhurst.

"I'll rust here," she muttered as she wrenched the car door open. As she slammed the door behind her, she remembered the car was still in Frank's name. She opened her purse and added "change car registration and insurance to my name" to her list. Something else nagged for her attention. Oh, yes, the house. She'd have to ask Frank about the house.

It all came rushing back, and Ellen leaned over the steering wheel, feeling weak and breathless. All her self-created confidence and bravado seemed gone. Hanging onto the wheel, Ellen blinked back tears.

"I will not cry," she told herself firmly. "I will not cry."

She straightened her back, her chin wobbling a little. Looking at her watch, she realized she had just enough time to drive across town to her next appointment.

Parking the car in front of the office complex, she walked in with her head high. She stopped in the restroom and brushed her hair quickly. She splashed cold water on her face before she remembered the makeup; then she had to scrub the rest off to make it look natural. Finally, she walked into the insurance office.

The receptionist—an overly made-up bleached blonde—looked at her with a superior smile. Ellen struggled to control her anger. Within a few minutes, a middle-aged woman came out and called her name.

"Please take a seat," she said, waving Ellen to a seat across from her desk. "I'm Katherine Brandt." Ellen shook her hand then sat down nervously. Katherine read her résumé carefully, then set it aside.

"Why are you looking for a job, Ellen?" she asked.

Her voice was so kind that Ellen felt tears rush to her eyes. Blinking them back, she tried to tell the truth as unemotionally as she could. "My husband and I are separating. I need a job."

Silence. Katherine looked at her kindly. "Do you have any office skills?"

Ellen smiled and drew herself up confidently. "Yes. I can type sixty words per minute, file, organize anything or anyone, and answer phones."

"Do you have computer skills?"

Ellen felt the confidence drain away. "No," she admitted. "But I can learn."

Katherine hesitated. "Well, we really need someone with Lotus experience."

Ellen felt her anger rise again. "If you just give me a chance, you'll find I'm a quick learner." She stopped herself before she added anything about the bleached blonde at the reception desk.

Katherine smiled. "Good. That's the enthusiasm and determination I'm looking for. Will you be willing to work for five dollars an hour?"

"Yes!" Ellen immediately responded. *How much would*

five dollars an hour bring in every month? She didn't stop to calculate.

Katherine smiled. "Great. When can you start?"

Ellen blinked and stammered. "Monday?"

"That sounds perfect," Katherine replied. "We'll start you on the typewriter, and you'll do phone backup for Mindi."

Ellen smiled and nodded. *Mindi must be the blonde*, she thought.

Katherine rose and shook her hand. "Monday then. Thank you for stopping in."

Ellen smiled and walked out of the office. She gave Mindi an equally condescending smile on her way out the door. She felt almost good on the way home. She had a job and her own bank accounts; things were going to be OK.

When she arrived home, the house was silent. She walked through and tried to ignore the loneliness of the place. A note waited for her on the bed. Frank's handwriting. Her heart beat faster. She tore it open with shaking hands.

> Ellen,
> Sorry I missed you. We need to talk about settlement and everything else. For now, you can keep the minivan, and I'll take the sedan. You can have the house. I came back and got more of my things. I'll be back for the rest next week.
> As you probably already know, I've quit my job with the church. I handed in my formal resignation this morning. Since I have another job already, I will send you monthly checks.
> Frank.

Ellen sank onto the bed and let her tears flow unchecked. When had their marriage deteriorated to who-gets-what?

It seemed so pathetic to be dividing up a lifetime of worthless belongings. Ellen remembered all the notes Frank had written to her. All the cute names he had called her. The way he always signed them "All my love, always, Frank." Now it was just signed "Frank."

His words came back. "I don't know if I ever loved you."

Ellen grabbed her pillow and sobbed. She felt an arm go around her shoulders, and she looked up to see Jeff sitting beside her. He held her, saying nothing, while she cried uncontrollably.

Chapter 3

"No, Mom, it's OK. God will work everything out." Ellen wiped her eyes as she spoke.

"Honey, are you sure? You can come down for a nice visit. Bring Jeff. I'm sure Frank will come to his senses soon." Her mother's voice sounded crushed and confused. "I just don't understand . . ."

Ellen squeezed her eyes shut, feeling a headache starting. "I don't either, Mom. But I start a job on Monday. We can't come and visit." Inside, Ellen knew a visit would only make things worse. She felt determined to handle the situation like a responsible adult. The breakdown she had the night before would not happen again. Period.

"Call anytime. Daddy and I will be praying that everything works out."

"Thanks, Mom. I love you."

"I love you too."

Ellen hung up the phone and felt sick inside. Mom and Dad didn't believe in divorce. When they married their only daughter to a pastor, they had believed that her future was secure. Ellen tried to push Frank out of her thoughts and turn back to Jeff, who sat at the kitchen table eating breakfast.

"So what'd Grandma say?" he asked, his mouth full of cereal.

"Don't speak with your mouth full," Ellen replied automatically. "She wants us to come out to visit, but Florida is too far to drive, and we can't afford the air fare. And with a new job, I won't have the time off."

Jeff nodded. "Good. Dad never did like her."

Ellen raised an eyebrow at him. "Where did you hear that? He likes her. He always has."

"He told me that, last time she was here," he replied.

Ellen sighed. It sounded like Jeff knew Frank better than she did. Had Frank told her anything over the last few years?

"Well, he was joking," she lied. "Now hurry up and finish your breakfast. You'll be late for school."

He spooned the last of the milk from the bottom of the bowl. "Are we going to go to church this weekend?" he asked.

Ellen pretended not to hear him as she busied herself by emptying the dishwasher. *Could she go? Would they understand? They always thought we had the perfect family. No*, she mentally corrected, *you always thought you had the perfect family*. She cringed as she imagined their response. No one from the church had called, even though Frank resigned two days before. She didn't doubt that it had already made news with every parishioner.

Jeff put his bowl in the dishwasher, grabbed his books, and disappeared out the back door. Ellen leaned against the counter, her head pounding. She longed to crawl back in bed, pull the covers over her head, and never reappear.

"Get a hold of yourself," she muttered, pulling herself up straight. "You come from stronger stock than this."

She grabbed her purse and backed the minivan out of the garage. She drove past the church, almost hoping to see Frank's car. It wasn't there, of course. She wondered, not for the first time, where he was staying, where he was working. The church brought back so many memories.

"Is this it?" she remembered herself saying sixteen years before as she first looked at the small, dumpy building.

"It may be small, but God needs us here," Frank had replied, his eyes shining. "We'll be happy here."

Ellen wiped tears away and drove from the church without a backward glance. *Frank, when did you lose your faith?* she mentally asked. *Where did we go wrong?* She thought of the years and the love they poured into that small congregation. She remembered the births, the baptisms, the weddings, and the deaths. They connected with all of it.

She pulled up in front of the grocery store and parked in the last available spot. It seemed like everyone in town was doing Friday shopping at the same time. Once inside, she grabbed a cart and started trying to maneuver it through crowded aisles. She automatically picked up Frank's favorite cereal before remembering. Setting it back on the shelf, she tried to fight the hopeless feeling inside. Why did everything feel so meaningless? She then grabbed Jeff's favorite cereal off the shelf and threw it into the cart. She looked at the things piled there and knew she had too much food.

"Jeff's a growing boy," she told herself as she pushed the cart down the aisle. Ahead of her, the church organist turned the corner. Ellen smiled. Dorothy was always one of her favorite people.

"Hi, Dorothy," she said.

Dorothy looked at her, then looked away. Ellen tried again.

"Hi, Dorothy."

Dorothy looked at her, pure hatred on her face. "You whore," she snarled, then pushed Ellen's cart out of the way with her cart. She disappeared around the corner, her ample hips twitching angrily.

Ellen stood still, stunned. *What had Frank told the*

church? Other shoppers stared at her with open curiosity. Her face flamed and tears started. Shoving the cart into a soft-drink display, she left it there and ran blindly out of the store. She sobbed as she fumbled with the key to the ignition.

"Why? Why? Why?" she screamed, pounding on the steering wheel. Tears ran down her face, unchecked. Her anger at Frank knew no bounds.

Arriving home, she pawed through his office, looking for any clue about where he might have gone. She dumped everything on the floor, not caring. In the back of the top drawer, she found the business card of a smart-looking realtor. The residential number was circled. Ellen checked her watch and decided the woman would probably be at her office.

"Maybe it's a start," she muttered, picking up the phone and dialing.

"Good afternoon, H. G. Realty," a sweet voice answered.

"Is Sandy Renton there?" Ellen held her breath.

"I'm sorry, she's left for lunch. May I take a message?"

"No, thank you." Ellen hung up, feeling sick.

Is she the one? Ellen wondered as she looked at the smiling black-and-white photo on the business card. She looked slick and brittle—and at least forty-five years old. Ellen looked at the address on the card and decided to go to the office herself. *If the woman doesn't know Frank, I can just play stupid*, Ellen reasoned. Climbing back into the van, she drove as fast as she dared.

Pulling up in front of the building, she searched the parking lot for Frank's car. It wasn't there. She backed out and parked on a side street where she could watch the parking lot. She remembered Frank's explaining his need for a real-estate licence.

"It's really the best thing," he'd told her. "When we get a new house, I'll be able to handle the transactions myself!"

And I believed him, Ellen thought. *I bought the entire story.*

After a few minutes, Frank's car pulled into the parking lot, and he stepped out. Another car pulled up beside him, and a woman got out. Ellen checked the business card in her hand. The picture looked a few years old, but it definitely was the same person. Ellen was just about ready to get out of the van and go up to Frank when he put an arm around the woman's waist.

"Liar!" Ellen screamed. Being too far away, no one heard her. She imagined gunning her minivan straight at Frank's sedan and ramming into the back bumper. She gripped the wheel and fantasized about the car flying over the curb and into the front of the building. She could imagine people rushing out the front door and gaping at her. Then she'd back up and dart back into traffic, feeling powerful and in control.

But instead, she sat quietly, shaking with shame and rage as Frank opened the door for the woman and disappeared into the real-estate office. Though trying to control the shaking in her body, Ellen could hardly start the engine of the van.

Don't do anything public, she told herself, breathing hard.

She pulled the minivan carefully into traffic. Her shaking hadn't stopped. Her rage rose uncontrollably.

I'm going to burn everything of his when I get home, she vowed, her face flaming. She caught her reflection in the rearview mirror and didn't recognize herself. Gone was the smooth, placid expression she always wore. Someone she barely recognized stared back at her.

She jerked the minivan to a stop in front of the house with a squeal. Jumping out, she didn't bother to drive it into the garage or lock it. She didn't care. A white anger she had never known before flamed through her. Ellen suddenly knew how people could commit crimes of passion.

She left the door open as she whipped through the house, gathering any of Frank's things she could find. Sweeping all his theological books off the bookshelves, she lugged them into the back yard and lighted them. Next, she cleared out the file cabinet. Everything had to go. Finally, she dragged out his box of sermons, and she fed them to the fire, one by one.

First, the sermon on trusting God. Then the sermon on the love of God. A wedding sermon. She tore that one up before she burned it. Ellen felt like she was burning all her hopes and all her beliefs with the sermons. And it wasn't until she dumped the last one on the flames that her anger started to subside.

It started to rain as the last of the papers burned to ashes. Ellen stood, sobbing and holding herself, oblivious to the weather.

"God, where are You?" she screamed.

No reply. The rain pelted harder.

"Are You dead, like the sermons I just burned?" Ellen cried. She sat on the ground, not caring that it was muddy.

Still no reply. Ellen tried to remember all the promises she'd ever been taught. She tried to sing some of the songs she had learned about Jesus. But nothing took the pain away. Cynically, she remembered all the pious advice she'd given people when they had lost their faith in God. Now she wondered if they'd known something she hadn't.

Thoroughly drenched, Ellen pulled herself up and walked stiffly toward the house, turning for one last look at the soggy, blackened mess.

From now on, I do it myself, she vowed. *If You can't keep Your promises, I'll go it alone.*

Ellen slammed the door behind her. And inside she knew she had shut off a part of herself.

Chapter 4

Ellen knocked loudly on Jeff's door. "Jeff?"

The music continued pounding. She tried again. "JEFF!"

The music stopped abruptly, and the door opened.

"What?" Jeff stared at her, annoyed.

Ellen put one hand to her pounding head. "The music," she said pointedly.

He shrugged. "Sorry." He sounded anything but.

Ellen let it pass. "You'll be late for school. You want me to drop you off on my way to work?"

"Nah. I'll just walk," he mumbled.

Ellen ached inside as she watched him gather his books. In less than a week, he had gone from being a happy, well-adjusted fifteen-year-old to a surly, uncommunicative boy she barely knew. "Be home by supper," Ellen called after him.

A slammed door answered her. She checked herself one more time in the mirror. She looked professional, in control. Only the tightness around her mouth betrayed her. That and the empty look in her eyes. She looked away quickly.

Grabbing her purse and keys, she backed the van slowly out of the driveway. As she drove past the street to Frank's real-estate office, she gripped the wheel and felt her stomach turn over. *Had it only been three days since she saw him*

33

*with that woman? Sandy. What a stupid name for a grown
woman*, Ellen thought bitterly.

She parked outside her office and entered the building
five minutes early. Katherine greeted her at the door with
a smile.

"Ellen, I'm glad you're here. Mindi called in sick today,
so I'll need you to cover the phones. OK?"

Ellen placed her purse on Mindi's desk and eyed the
complicated-looking phone system. "Sure," she replied
uneasily.

Katherine patted her on the back. "You'll do fine. Come
get me if you have any questions." She turned to go, then
turned back to her. "Oh, I've already unforwarded them, so
you won't need to worry about that."

Ellen blinked. *Unforwarded?* "OK," she said.

She sat down and stared at the system of buttons and
lights. The phone at the church had been an ordinary-
looking phone, much like hers at home. This one seemed to
stare menacingly back at her, its lights looking like cold
eyes.

Ring!

One of the lights lighted up, and Ellen lifted the receiver
carefully and answered. It rang again in her ear. Franti-
cally she began hitting buttons on the phone board. It kept
ringing, then stopped.

Ring!

Ring!

Two of the lights lighted up, and ringers seemed to be
coming from everywhere. She got one answered and put
through to Katherine; then the other lines lighted up
again.

"Good morning, State Farm Insurance, can you hold?"

"No!" the voice barked. "I already got cut off once. Put me
through!"

Ellen felt tears welling. The other lines started ringing

insistently. She put the caller on hold, put her face in her hands, and sobbed, the phones ringing wildly around her. Katherine appeared at her side, quietly answered all the calls, took messages, then sat on the corner of the desk. Ellen felt mortified.

"I'm sorry," she sniffled. "You'll probably want to fire me now."

Katherine gave her a compassionate smile. "Let's forward the phones to the answering service for a few minutes," she said. She dialed a few numbers, and the board went silent. "Come, we'll talk in my office."

Ellen followed her, feeling sick to her stomach. After only one day on the job, she was going to be fired. She sat down numbly across the desk from Katherine. Katherine handed her a box of tissues, and Ellen fought another wave of tears.

"Ellen, let me tell you something about myself," she began quietly. "Five years ago my husband and I split. I had no training, no work experience. No one would hire me. Now, I have my own insurance office, and I make triple what that jerk does."

Ellen listened, her tears stopped.

"What I'm trying to say is that I've been where you are. I expect you to take time to learn. If you don't understand something, just ask me." She smiled slightly. "Before you try tackling it."

Ellen managed a small smile. "I will, I promise."

Katherine looked at her a second. "How long have you and your husband been . . ."

Ellen lowered her eyes. "A week," she answered painfully. *A week? Was it only a week? Why did it feel like a year or more?*

Katherine sighed. "Men are pigs."

"Absolutely," Ellen agreed bitterly.

Katherine looked at her watch. "Well, let's get you trained on the phones."

Ellen stood and followed Katherine out to the reception desk. After five minutes, the buttons and lights didn't seem as confusing. As Katherine turned to go back into her office, she smiled again at Ellen.

"You'll be fine," she reassured her.

"Thanks," Ellen replied gratefully.

The morning passed quickly. On her lunch hour, Ellen walked down the street to a bookstore and browsed through the self-help section. She had never looked in this section before. Now, every book seemed to be written just for her. She pulled one off the shelf about women who love too much and the men who hate them. She shuddered and put it back. Another beckoned. And another. She bought three of them. One on surviving divorce, one on getting back the man you love, and one that claimed infidelity can help a marriage.

Taking the bag from the clerk, Ellen stepped back onto the sidewalk. Sun struggled through the clouds, lighting the shabby streets and making them look more cheerful than usual. She had walked half a block toward the office when she saw John Stone, one of Frank's church members, coming her way. Dorothy's angry words came back to her, and she panicked. She looked for somewhere, anywhere, to hide.

Turning abruptly, she bumped into another pedestrian and started running blindly down the street. Her high heels slipped dangerously on the damp pavement. She skidded around a corner, barely holding her balance.

"Ellen!" John called after her. "Ellen."

Ellen stopped, out of breath and embarrassed for being caught trying to hide. John caught up with her. Ellen refused to meet his eyes and steeled herself for his attack.

"Ellen, we missed you in church last week. Are you doing OK?" His voice sounded warm and concerned.

Ellen blinked back tears and cautiously raised her eyes

to his. "I . . . uh . . . well, you know," she finished lamely.

He nodded, seeming to understand. "You're welcome back any time, Ellen. You have friends there."

Ellen's eyes shimmered. "Thanks."

John's lined face looked kind, and he visibly struggled for something to say. Ellen felt a rush of gratefulness to him. He'd always been one of the quiet, grandfatherly types who sat in the back of the church and never said much.

"I, um, think Jeff and I will be going to the Park Rapids Church," she told him. Ellen knew it was a lie, but figured he wouldn't bother to check it out.

John looked relieved. "Well, if there's anything you need, like something done around the house or anything, let me know."

Ellen smiled again, this time genuinely. "Thank you, John. That means so much to me."

He looked embarrassed, shuffled his feet a little. "Well, see you later."

"Later."

Ellen stood and watched him stride back down the street. He had the walk of an old cowboy, she decided. Long-legged and loping. She turned back toward her office. So, she had friends at the church. She tried to think of the congregation individually rather than en masse like she always had before. Friends. No, she had never considered them friends even when she and Frank pastored them. They were the flock. She couldn't remember ever talking to any of them as friends.

"I've been carefully schooled," Ellen muttered to herself as she stopped and blankly stared at a window display.

She remembered the senior pastor's wife in their first church pulling her aside and telling her the rules of the job.

"Always dress conservatively, always smile, never up-stage your husband, and never make friends with members of your congregation."

"Why?" Ellen had asked.

"Stirs up jealousy. And you can never really trust them."

Ellen shook her head and walked on. *Friends in the congregation.* As she opened the door to the office, she realized she had no real friends in the entire town. She had talked only to Frank or her mother.

Ellen pushed all thoughts of the church and Frank out of her mind for the rest of the afternoon. She typed, filed, answered the phone, and took messages for Katherine. By five, she felt she really understood the phone system. She drove home slowly, not wanting to face an empty house.

Maybe I should get a dog, she thought as she turned into the driveway. The lights were on in the house. She got out of the van quickly, thinking Jeff had brought some of his friends home from school.

She walked in the kitchen door. Frank sat at the table, looking like he always had. Ellen felt her stomach drop.

"What are you doing here?" she asked. Her voice sounded strange, hollow somehow.

He smiled at her. "I just wanted to go over a few things with you. Where have you been?"

"A job." Ellen raised an eyebrow at him. "I have to work and support a family now." *You pig, you jerk,* she raged inwardly. She kept remembering his arm around the real-estate woman's waist.

He blushed. "I'll be sending you support money."

Ellen dumped her purse on the counter. "How long, Frank? How long have you been slutting around?"

He tried to misunderstand. "I don't know what you're talking about."

"Liar! I saw you. She's a real-estate woman, and her name is Sandy. Don't lie to me. What do you think I am? Stupid?" Ellen could feel her face flushing hotter and hotter as she spat out the words.

Frank looked down quickly. "I never wanted to hurt you."

Ellen gripped the back of one of the dining-room chairs. "Answer my question. How long?"

"A year," he muttered.

"How did you meet her?"

"Came in for counseling . . ." He looked away.

Ellen felt the anger drain away and a dead, hopeless feeling take its place. "Do you love her?" she whispered.

He shrugged. "Yes. No. I don't know."

Ellen, sensing a softening in him, gripped one of Frank's hands. "Let's go away for a while. Let's try to work this out." She mentally pushed Sandy out of her mind.

He shook his head. "It's too late."

Ellen sat numbly as he spread papers in front of her. Legal papers. Legal separation. Divorce petition. It all seemed so fast.

". . . of course, I'll be wanting visitation rights for Jeff. I figured he could spend weekends with me. Or, if you want, part of the week . . ."

Frank's voice seemed to fade in and out. *What did Sandy have?* Ellen wondered. *Why did he want her?* She tried to remember what the woman looked like. Ash-blond hair. Medium build. Sharp facial features.

"Who else?" she said suddenly, interrupting Frank's words.

"What?"

"Who else have you been with?" she asked, starting to feel nauseated.

"No one," he assured her.

Ellen shook her head. "Frank, if there's anyone else, I need to know. Now."

"Ellen, there's been no one else. I promise."

"What about her?" Ellen choked out. "Does the whore have a long sexual history?"

Frank drew up angrily. "I will not have you talking about her that way. She's not a whore!"

"Well, what else do you call a woman who sleeps with a married man?" she snapped.

Frank clenched and unclenched his fists, obviously trying to control himself. "It's obvious we're not getting anywhere tonight. I'll call and continue this discussion later. My address and phone numbers are by the phone."

Ellen sat staring at the papers in front of her as Frank stood up and grabbed his car keys.

"By the way," he asked as he turned to leave. "What did you do with all my books and things?"

Ellen turned and gave him a mock sweet smile. "There was a fire. It was an accident. Really."

He turned and stormed out of the house, slamming the door behind him. Ellen dissolved into tears. Rocking slightly, she hugged herself as she cried.

She'd always been a good girl. She and Frank had married as virgins. She'd always looked at the scourge of sexual diseases with a feeling of superiority. She knew it could never happen to her. Now she shuddered, thinking of Frank with her, Frank with that woman, that woman with who-knows-how-many other men. She fought a wave of nausea.

Sniffling, she stood up and grabbed her purse off the kitchen counter. Opening her date book, she wrote "Make doctor's appointment" at the top of her to-do list.

The pain came back and she cried again. The documents blurred in front of her. She clutched the sides of the table tightly as if it, too, would disappear.

Chapter 5

The dream came again. She and Frank walking down the beach on their honeymoon, holding hands. Frank brushing the hair out of her eyes and telling her she was beautiful. Ellen knew, as she kissed him, that he loved her and that he always would.

She woke with tears on her cheeks. The clock read 4:00 a.m. The bed felt huge and lonely. She rolled over and clutched the extra pillow to her stomach, mulling the relationship over and over in her mind. The dreams and the early morning ruminating had become a nightly ritual. And on the weekends when Jeff went to Frank's, it seemed to get worse.

I should have been more loving, Ellen told herself. *And I should have worked harder to get those extra pounds off.* She touched her hips. Since Frank left a month ago, she had lost fifteen pounds. Her clothes hung tentlike on her emaciated frame. She sighed and rolled onto her back, still holding the pillow. Maybe if Frank saw how thin she was now, he'd want to get back together.

She pushed the thought away as soon as it formulated. But it persisted. She imagined the scenario. A problem to discuss with Frank. They'd meet in a restaurant. Ellen would wear his favorite dress. He would be unable to stop looking at her. He'd say he made a mistake and couldn't they please try again. Ellen felt a stab of hope. *God could work it out, couldn't He?*

"God, are You there?" she quietly whispered.

No answer. She didn't expect one. But each time, somewhere inside she hoped that He would answer.

God wants us together, she reasoned. She thought of the self-help books she'd been reading. All of them said to give the man time. That he's just going through a midlife crisis. As Ellen thought of Frank's gentle smile, the way his eyes crinkled in the corners, and his soft hair, she missed him so badly she ached inside.

I should have listened to him more. I should have been watching better. Maybe I could have caught the affair sooner—before it went too far. She turned over again, punching the pillow in frustration. Her head was beginning to ache.

When she'd gone in for her doctor's appointment two weeks before, the doctor had reassured her she had no diseases and that she should start getting out more to combat the loneliness and depression. She even suggested dating. Ellen shuddered at the thought of dating. She saw Frank in every man she met. She saw Frank when she went to sleep and when she woke up. The numbness she had for the first week or so after he left had worn off, and now a cold, empty, aching loneliness filled her.

"I never loved anyone else," she whispered, staring at the ceiling. She remembered meeting him in college. She, a vivacious English major, he a shy theology student. They had collaborated on a religious program at the college and never stopped seeing each other after that.

Were there clues, even back then? Ellen wondered. She thought of the hours he had spent studying Greek and Hebrew. His homework, the church, everything else came before their relationship. They married as virtual strangers. Ellen always assumed that was the way all pastors related to their wives.

She looked at the clock again. 4:50 a.m. Ellen couldn't remember how the time had passed. It seemed to have disappeared.

"Now I know why people drink," she muttered to herself as she unwrapped her legs from the tangled bedcovers.

She got out of bed and paced to the window. The street sat silent and dark. No cars drove by. No lights warmed any of the other houses on the street. It was Saturday morning. And already Ellen wished the day was through.

She didn't mind the workdays as much. With somewhere to go and something to fill so many hours, she felt they passed quickly. She threw on a robe and turned on the TV. Most of the stations were off the air. One had continual news. She flicked the TV off again, shuddering at the silence in the house.

Ellen padded to the kitchen and made herself a cup of tea. Outside, the darkness started slowly turning to gray. She looked at the calendar on the wall. March fifth. Was it already a month since Frank had moved out? She wondered how the distant past of seventeen years could seem closer than a month ago.

Ellen finished her tea, rinsed out the cup, and opened the living-room curtains. Glancing at the porch, she noticed a white envelope lying in front of the door. Wrapping her robe tighter around her, she opened the door and picked up the envelope.

Her name was written in crude lettering across the front of the envelope. The envelope had no postage or address. Ellen closed the door against the early morning chill and sat on the sofa. She stared at the envelope a minute. Somewhere, inside, she knew she didn't want to read it. She took a deep breath, opened the envelope, and unfolded the letter.

Dear Ellen,

You are a sinner. You have sinned against God and against the church. Don't you know what the Bible says about divorce? You are a disgrace to our entire congregation.

Don't bother coming back. We want church members our young people can look up to. Hopefully you can find it in your heart to repent to God.

A concerned party.

Angrily Ellen wadded the paper and threw it on the floor. It lay crumpled in the middle of the carpet, but Ellen could still see the words burning in front of her.

"A concerned party," Ellen muttered. "Didn't even have the nerve to sign a name!"

She grabbed the paper off the floor and opened it again. Could she recognize the handwriting? She studied the sloppy scrawl. No, it looked like it had been written with the wrong hand.

All hail the church! Ellen seethed, getting off the sofa and marching into the kitchen. Grabbing a book of matches, she burned the letter and the envelope in the sink. It was consumed quickly, but her anger blazed on. She strode around the house, trying to think of someone to call, of something to say.

Angrily, she remembered how some in the congregation had fawned over her, each one wanting her opinion on this person or that person. Now they judged.

Why can't they understand? This isn't my fault!

She thought of some of the church members Frank had chastised because of infidelity. She remembered one woman in particular. Pat. Pat left her husband; then her son died of AIDS. The church was scandalized.

So were you, Ellen reminded herself. She suddenly wondered if she had judged too quickly. She pushed the thought out of her mind. She had never written a nasty letter to anyone. She had always shown people their wrongdoings with Christian love and compassion.

The walls of the house seemed to close in on her as she paced back and forth. By seven o'clock, she knew she couldn't spend the day in the house.

"I've got to get out of this town," she muttered as she paced the living room.

The words of the letter came back, and she fought angry tears.

"I gave my life for that church!" she said angrily, wiping at the tears. She remembered the years she spent attending meetings, hostessing parties, coordinating weddings.

"Why? Why? Why?" Her voice bounced off the walls and echoed back at her.

She knew she couldn't stay in the house another minute. Throwing on jeans and a sweat shirt, she backed the van out of the garage and got on I-84 heading west. She had a vague idea of going to Portland or maybe the beach. Each mile that separated her made her feel freer. She didn't see the scenery. She concentrated on keeping her speed up and her mind clear.

Ellen stopped in Portland for gas and food. It still didn't feel far enough away. She got back in the van and kept going. The freeway turned into a two-lane road that wound through the coast range. Finally she arrived in Cannon Beach. She grabbed a sandwich at a deli and walked down to the beach. As she sat watching the waves roll in, she could feel her tension and anger finally draining away. Only the pain remained.

"Why?" she asked again, this time quietly.

A couple walked past, holding hands and smiling at each other. The woman tripped over a piece of driftwood, and the man caught her around the waist, steadying her. Ellen, watching, caught her breath in pain.

You used to look at me like that, she mentally said to Frank. *We used to hang on to each other, helping each other along. When did we stop?*

Ellen hugged herself against the wind. The waves crashed in closer and closer. The tide was coming in. She stood up and walked slowly down the beach. She wanted to walk straight into the waves and never come back.

"Would anyone miss me?" she wondered aloud.

She was afraid to answer her own question. She stood and silently watched the waves. And as the gray light finally started to fade, she turned and walked back into town. She stopped in at a bookstore and bought a cheap paperback romance.

"Are there any good bed and breakfasts in town?" Ellen asked the clerk as he rang up her book.

He scratched his head. "Would you like a list?"

Ellen nodded. "Also, any motels you'd recommend."

He handed her a list of lodgings. Ellen thanked him and walked out of the store. She found a pay phone and started dialing the motels first. She found a vacancy at one of the first beach-front places she called.

She drove by a market first and picked up a toothbrush and other sundry essentials, then parked in front of the motel. Ellen could hear the waves crashing as she got out of the van. She got her key from a bored-looking desk clerk.

I wonder what he thinks of me, checking in without luggage, Ellen thought, smiling.

She shut the door behind her and walked straight to the window. Her room was on the ground floor. She opened the curtains and pulled a chair over in front of the sliding-glass door. The waves looked so close she almost wanted to reach out and grab them.

The light faded completely outside, and the motel floodlights flicked on. The light splashed eerily off the waves. Ellen sat, still staring.

"What if I don't go back?" she whispered.

She had heard about people who disappeared out of their lives. No one would care. Frank wouldn't care. The church wouldn't care. She thought of the letter again, and her stomach tightened. Jeff. For all her wishing, Ellen knew she couldn't leave Jeff.

She pulled her to-do list out of her purse and uncapped her pen. *Leaving Riverhurst was the best thing I could have done today*, she thought as she stared at the blank notebook page.

"I should keep a journal," she said. She remembered keeping one all the way through college, then again when Jeff was a baby. She wrote "Buy a journal" across the top of her list.

The next things were easy. "Sell the house." Find a new job in—" Here she stopped. Where should she move? Portland? She thought of the dreary gray city with its frantic drivers and shook her head No. Seattle? No better. Eugene? She carefully considered each possibility, but every one seemed wrong somehow.

"I'm running away," Ellen muttered. Even as she said the words, she realized she wasn't trying to run away from Riverhurst or even from the church, but rather from herself. She wanted to keep going and going until she could leave the pain behind and start over as a new person.

She imagined hopping on a plane to Europe or the Caribbean and never coming back. She could wait on tables and fall in love with a gorgeous Greek waiter like the woman in the movie *Shirley Valentine*. But even as she schemed, Ellen knew she couldn't leave.

Ellen put the list down and stared bleakly at the waves. Inside she knew she wouldn't sell the house. She knew she wouldn't go somewhere and start over. She'd go back home the next day and be what everyone wanted her to be.

She knew she couldn't let go of Frank either. If she left

and moved to a new city, she'd always wonder what he was doing. She would lose any chance of winning him back.

Ellen sat up straight, feeling hopeful again. Maybe she could get him back. Maybe he just needed some time to think. She knew he didn't love that woman. He just couldn't find any other way to get out of the church.

"That's it," she whispered. "I'll go back home and work on my marriage. I am not a quitter. Then when we get back together, we can leave town as a family."

She thought of how exhausted Frank would be each night after spending days with church members. *He just needed to get away from the church*, she told herself. *There's no good in the church. It destroyed him, and now the members are out to get me. If we can get away together, everything will be perfect again.*

She stood up and closed the curtains, a smile on her face. Inside, Ellen felt like a huge weight had been lifted. For the first time in weeks, she had a direction. Taking off her jeans, she slid into bed and opened the paperback novel.

"Thank You, God, for pointing me in the direction You want me to go," she whispered.

Chapter 6

Ellen sat in Portland International Airport, waiting for her mother's plane to land. She sat as far from the smoking section as possible, but the smoke drifted over and made her sneeze. She clenched a tissue in her hand and glared at the smokers who blew smoke in every direction.

"Flight 351 from Chicago is arriving at gate 9C."

Ellen looked at her watch. The plane was late. She stood and walked over to the gate. Outside, the May sunshine glinted off the shiny plane. She remembered trying to put off the visit. Finally, three months after the separation, Mom won.

The passengers started coming out of the tunnel. Ellen stood back and let other people greet their friends and family. She knew Mom would be one of the last ones off the plane. Someone jostled against her with a flight bag.

"Excuse me," Ellen mumbled automatically. The businessman didn't respond.

Finally she saw Mom's gray head toward the end of the stream of people. The flight attendant walked beside her. Ellen waved to get her attention.

"Hi, sweetie!" Mom said as she dropped her carry-on bag on the floor and gave Ellen a hug.

Ellen hugged her back. The flight attendant turned to leave, but Mom stopped her.

N.T.T.—4

"Cynthia, this is my daughter Ellen I told you about. Ellen, this is Cynthia. She was so nice to me all the way from Chicago. I had to switch planes there, you see, and the O'Hare Airport always makes my ulcer flare up. . . ."

Mom kept talking. Ellen grinned at the flight attendant and shrugged her shoulders. The flight attendant smiled back, as if to say "I know; I have one too." Ellen picked up Mom's carry-on bag and backed off a few steps.

". . . And, Cynthia, honey, you just keep trying with that pilot of yours." Mom patted the flight attendant's arm. "You're too beautiful to be single."

The flight attendant thanked her, and Ellen took her mother's arm, still smiling.

"Come on, Mom. It's a long drive home."

Ellen guided Mom down the corridor toward the baggage claim area. Mom kept talking, and Ellen listened, letting her mother's familiar voice take her back years.

". . . so wish your father would fly out, but you know how he is with planes . . ."

While they waited for Mom's suitcases, Ellen gave her a hug. "I'm so glad you came out."

Mom smiled, but her eyes filled with tears. "I just wish it could be under better circumstances."

Ellen sighed. "Me too."

They reached the van, and Ellen piled all the luggage in the back. After paying the parking fee, they got on I-205 south. Mom stared out the windows.

"It's sunny here," she announced. "I thought it always rained."

Ellen laughed and signaled on to I-84 east. "You're used to being here in the winter. Sometimes we get nice summers. You'd think it was Florida without the humidity," she teased.

Mom flashed her a grin. "Yeah, but we get sunshine year round."

"And humidity and smog and hurricanes," Ellen teased

back, enjoying their age-old battle. Ever since Ellen had left home, they'd battled about whose state was better— theirs or hers.

"But we have fresh oranges, warm beaches." Mom looked out the window at the gorge. She seemed to have lost interest in the conversation. "Do you hear from him?" she asked.

Ellen gripped the wheel tighter. "Yes. We talk about every two weeks. Mostly about Jeff. Jeff is having a rough time," Ellen explained. She tried to make her voice light. Inside, she felt that sick feeling she always felt when she thought of Jeff.

"Have you met her?" Mom asked, not looking at Ellen.

Ellen gritted her teeth. "Yes. I met her a month ago. Frank thought it would be a good thing to be friends. For Jeff's sake."

She thought of the awkward meeting in a restaurant. Sandy too friendly and made-up. Frank refusing to meet her eyes. Ellen slowly shredding paper napkin after paper napkin in her lap.

Silence. They passed the exit for Multnomah Falls.

"Did you have a nice flight?" Ellen asked, trying to change the subject.

"Wonderful. They gave me a special vegetarian plate."

Ellen smiled. "I told you they would."

Mom smiled and looked out the window again. Ellen looked at her, amazed at how much she'd aged. Her usually spry five-foot frame looked shrunken and tired now. Ellen felt a twinge of guilt, knowing her breakup with Frank weighed heavily on Mom.

"How's your job going?" Mom asked.

"Great. That's the best thing. Katherine—that's my boss—thinks I should get my insurance license. She thinks I'd be a wonderful salesperson." Ellen pulled into the left lane and passed a slow-moving RV.

"You get that from your father." Mom gripped the sides of the seat and eyed the speedometer. Ellen slowed down a little. "Even when you were a kid, you got the most money in Ingathering."

Ellen smiled. "I did, didn't I?"

The miles then passed quickly as they remembered stories from Ellen's childhood. Ellen noticed they avoided any mention of Frank. She squinted at the sign for Park Rapids and hoped Mom wouldn't want to go to church the next day.

"Will you want to go to church tomorrow?" she asked casually.

Mom looked shocked. "Of course!"

Ellen groaned inside. "I just thought with your flight and everything you might be too tired. . . ."

Mom shook her head emphatically. "I'm not *that* old yet!"

Ellen smiled and passed another car. Inside she shook. She hadn't entered a church since Frank had left. She had no more desire to see church members than they wanted to see her.

"I'll take you to the Park Rapids Church," she said out loud.

They reached Riverhurst, and Ellen parked the van and honked the horn for Jeff. He came out and helped Mom out of the car.

"Grandma! Good to see you!" He hugged her tightly and kissed both her cheeks.

Ellen stared, open-mouthed. Jeff hadn't been this friendly for months. She shrugged. Maybe he's getting over it.

"Jeff! I swear you've grown a foot since I saw you last. How tall are you?" Mom squeezed his arm. "And look at these muscles."

Jeff puffed up. "I'm nearly six feet!" he bragged. "And I work out every day. And I windsurf."

"WindSURF?" She looked at Ellen, confused.

Ellen smiled. "Kind of like sailing on a surfboard."

Jeff rolled his eyes. "It's much harder than that."

Ellen hid a smile. "Oh, well, sorry. Why don't you use your muscles to get Grandma's bags out of the back."

Jeff walked around the back of the van, and Ellen led Mom inside the house. She stopped inside the living room and surveyed it.

"It's exactly the same," she accused. "Why haven't you changed anything?"

Ellen blinked and looked at the living room for what felt like the first time. "I don't know," she replied truthfully. "I guess I haven't had the energy."

She thought of the first dark month after Frank left. It was all she could do to get out of bed, shower, and brush her teeth in the morning.

She led Mom to the guest room and pointed out her towels in the bathroom. Ellen returned to the living room and stared at it. Yes, it definitely needed a change. *The whole house needs a change*, she thought. *It looks like it's just waiting for him to come home.*

Aren't you? Ellen asked herself. The pain came back in a rush. *Yes*, she admitted. *I'm waiting. Jeff's waiting. The whole house is waiting.*

She turned and walked into the kitchen. Leaning against the sink, she fought tears. She felt an arm go around her waist, and she jumped.

"It's OK, sweetie, it's just me," Mom said.

Ellen nodded. "I'm glad you're here," she whispered.

Mom turned her gently and wrapped her arms around her. Ellen felt something snap inside. Burying her face in that loving shoulder, she cried uncontrollably. Mom patted her on the back and cried with her.

"I've tried everything," Ellen sobbed. "I've tried to get him back. I've done everything all the books say. It doesn't work. I'm sorry, Mama. I'm sorry."

Mom shook her gently. "You have nothing to be sorry for. This is not your fault."

Ellen shook her head, wishing she could believe it. "It always takes two to break up a marriage. Frank says . . ."

While Mom waited for her to continue, she took Ellen's arm and led her to the sofa.

"Frank says he left because I was too demanding," Ellen whispered. Her breath came in ragged gasps.

Mom smoothed the hair off Ellen's face. "It was his decision to have an affair. It was his decision to leave. That is not your fault."

Ellen nodded and hugged Mom again. "I'm so glad you're here. The last three months have been horrible. . . ."

Mom hugged her close. "That's what mothers are for. You know I'll always be here for you."

The back screen door slammed, and Ellen straightened. Jeff came into the living room and stood awkwardly by the sofa.

"I put Grandma's things in her room," he said, looking at his feet.

"We'll be eating soon," Ellen told him.

He turned and walked into his bedroom, shutting the door behind him. Ellen tried to inject cheerfulness into her voice.

"So, lasagna sound good for supper?" she asked brightly.

Mom smiled, her eyes still worried. "Perfect."

Early the next morning, Ellen knocked on Jeff's door. He didn't answer.

"Jeff?"

No answer. She opened the door a crack. He lay sprawled across the bed, feet sticking out of the covers. He looked so vulnerable that Ellen longed to hug him. Instead, she shook his arm.

"Jeff. Time to get up."

He opened his eyes. "What time is it?"

"Eight. Get up. We're going to church with Grandma."

Jeff groaned and pulled the covers over his head. Ellen pulled them back down.

"Get up. I'm not leaving this room until you're out of bed."

He groaned again. "Why do we have to go?" he mumbled.

Good question, Ellen thought to herself. "Because I said so," she said out loud.

He sat up and rubbed his eyes. "Why not just tell her the truth? Will she really mind if we don't go to church anymore?"

Ellen felt sick inside at that comment. "It's not that we don't go to church; we just haven't gone for a while."

"Since Dad left," Jeff finished for her. He looked at her, his gaze sarcastic. Ellen knew he saw right to the hypocritic core. She turned away.

"Breakfast will be ready in a half an hour," she told him.

They drove to church in silence. Ellen could feel herself winding tighter and tighter inside as she parked the van in the church parking lot. She felt nauseated. Slowly she unwound her fingers from the steering wheel and pasted a fake smile on her face. She wanted to die, to shrink up and blow away—anything but walk into that church.

"I can't go in," she whispered.

Mom took her arm and gently propelled her through the front door. Ellen smiled woodenly at people. The pastor shook her hand.

"Ellen. I'm so glad you're here." He stopped, seeming to search for something to say.

Ellen didn't respond. The pastor's wife turned to another member and started talking. Ellen knew what she was doing. She remembered using the same tactics herself to avoid talking to certain people.

They think it's catching, Ellen thought grimly as she followed Jeff and her mother into the sanctuary. *Everyone thinks I'm catching.*

She thought of the times members of her congregation had divorced. Wives clung closer to their husbands when the divorced woman came around. Husbands tried to pretend nothing had happened, but the awkward pauses in conversations always gave them away.

They sat in the back. As the organ played familiar hymns, Ellen clenched her teeth tightly, knowing it would give her a headache for the rest of the day, but not caring.

The service seemed interminable. A sermon on how to know God's will in your life. Ellen wanted to laugh out loud. She remembered thinking it was God's will she and Frank get back together. She cringed as she remembered her stupid attempts to get him back. The fake emergency, friendship, ignoring him—Frank saw through them all, of course.

When the service ended, Ellen pushed her way out of the church. She stood, breathing heavily, on the front lawn as Jeff went back to the van and sulked. Mom took her time, greeting everyone on the way out.

"Ellen!"

Ellen turned and saw Pat, one of Frank's former members, coming toward her. She tried to smile.

"Hello, Pat."

Pat smiled warmly. "It's so good to see you here."

Ellen looked around, embarrassed. Pat, with her messy divorce and her son dying of AIDS. Pat, who refused to get the idea that no one wanted her in church anymore. Ellen looked at the ground and blushed. *Don't think we're soul mates now*, she said silently.

"It's good to be here," Ellen lied.

Pat looked at her searchingly. "Are you OK?"

Ellen drew herself up proudly. No one would see her cry. No one. Especially not Pat. "I'm fine, thank you."

Pat's expression showed she didn't believe Ellen. "If you ever need to talk, call me, OK?"

Ellen nodded and smiled. "I will, thank you."

She turned and stalked back to the van. *Pat. She won't leach on to me*, she thought angrily. She was to blame for her situation. She had left her husband. *I'm the one in the right here. I don't need her thinking I'm some kind of kindred spirit or something.*

She got into the van and angrily tapped the steering wheel. Jeff sat in the back, still sulking.

"I missed a bogus morning of wind," Jeff complained.

"Too bad," Ellen snapped.

Silence. Mom worked her way through the crowd and opened the van door. After the buckling of seat belts, Ellen backed out of the parking lot, spinning gravel in her haste.

"Everyone there seems so nice. Do you go there every week?" Mom's question sounded innocent, but Ellen knew better.

"No, Mom. I prefer not to go at all. Are you shocked? Well, now you know. I didn't tell you about the hate mail I started getting after Frank left. Church people are horrible, mean, and petty people. I want nothing more to do with them!" She spat the words out.

Mom didn't react. Ellen waited for the anger, braced herself against the inevitable lecture. It never came.

"Not all of them," Mom countered quietly.

Ellen shrugged. "I'm afraid I don't want to stay around to find a few pearls in all the mud."

Jeff sat very quiet in the back. Mom said nothing. Ellen pulled off the freeway and parked in front of the house.

"I'm sorry if I hurt you," she mumbled.

Mom shook her head. "It's not me, it's you. I'm worried about you."

"Yeah. So am I."

They walked into the house. Mom sat on the bed, watching Ellen change out of her church clothes.

"I promise I won't say anything after today, but I have to say what's on my mind, OK?"

Ellen nodded.

"This is exactly what the devil wants you to do. Yes, you've been hurt. Yes, those people are in the wrong. Yes, you need time to heal. But don't close yourself off with bitterness. Let God work on your pain."

Ellen bit back an angry reply about God. She didn't dare tell Mom she lay awake every night, staring at the ceiling and cursing God, hoping she could die. Instead, she walked over and gave Mom a quick kiss.

"I won't close myself off," she lied. "Thank you."

Mom grabbed her hand. "I'll be praying for you."

This softened Ellen's anger a little. *What could that hurt? Maybe God likes Mom better than He likes me*, she reasoned.

"Thanks."

Late that night as she lay on her back, staring at the ceiling, Ellen remembered her mother's words. She ached to believe, but she knew she couldn't go back. She couldn't go back to the church or to the safe, happy religion she'd always practiced. Both had been blown apart for her the moment Frank had walked out the door.

God? Do You care? Are You up there?

No reply. Ellen knew there wouldn't be one. Rolling over, she punched a pillow. Hard. The clock read two-thirty. She sighed and tried to sleep.

Chapter 7

Ellen arrived home late after taking her mother back to the airport. *We had a good week together,* Ellen decided as she unlocked the back door and quietly let herself into the house. She tiptoed through the dark kitchen. The clock read 1:15 a.m. She opened the refrigerator door and briefly considered making herself a sandwich. Knowing the bread was a little stale, she closed the door with a sigh. Taking off her shoes, she walked silently to Jeff's bedroom door and opened it a crack.

Moonlight fell across the bed, highlighting Jeff—his arm wrapped around a dark-haired girl. Ellen stood, stunned, trying to decide what to do. The girl sighed and snuggled closer to Jeff. The covers slid down, revealing the girl's bare shoulders. Ellen felt her face growing hot, and she flicked the light switch on angrily.

They sat up quickly, blinking in the sudden light. The girl blushed, but Jeff held her gaze, his eyes defiant.

"What are you doing, barging into my room?" he demanded.

Ellen gritted her teeth and prayed for control. "I want to see you in the living room. Now."

Jeff's gaze wavered a moment.

"Now!" She looked at the girl, cowering with the covers up to her chin. She looked no older than fifteen herself.

"You can get your clothes on and wait in the kitchen. I'll take you home."

Ellen turned and marched back to the living room. She paced angrily, waiting for Jeff to appear. When he did, he lounged against the wall nonchalantly and looked at her like she had lost all reason. The girl slunk to the kitchen. Ellen drew herself up icily. "When I get back, I want you up and waiting for me. Is that clear?" She glared at Jeff.

Jeff's confidence looked a little shaken. He looked at the floor. "Sure," he mumbled.

Grabbing her keys, Ellen led the girl to the car. The girl climbed in quietly, cringing against the door.

"Where do you live?" Ellen asked tightly.

"On the hill. Oak Street." She whispered the words.

Ellen squealed the car out of the driveway and sped angrily through the dark street of town. The girl started crying. Ellen thought she deserved the embarrassment.

"I'm really sorry," the girl whispered. "I didn't know . . ."

Ellen felt a twinge of pity despite her anger. She looked at the girl, who hunched dejectedly close to the door.

"How old are you?" Ellen asked quietly. She signaled and turned onto Oak Street. "Which house?"

The girl pointed at a small house on the corner. "Fourteen," she whispered.

Ellen stopped the car and turned to the girl. "You are too young to be fooling around with sex," she said bluntly.

The girl nodded and started crying. "We didn't 'do it,' we just, um . . ."

Ellen shook her head. "What's your name?"

"Megan."

"Megan, I want you to listen to me. No guy is worth messing up your future for. No one. Not even my son. Got it?"

Megan nodded. "Can I go now?"

Ellen sighed. "Yes."

She felt helpless as the girl climbed out of the van and ran to her house. She was sure Megan hadn't listened to anything she'd said. The helpless feeling turned to anger as Ellen pulled out of the driveway and headed home. The closer she got, the angrier she got.

She parked with a squeal and slammed the door as she entered the house. Jeff sat at the kitchen table, eating a bowl of cold cereal.

Ellen slammed her keys on the table and stood over him, breathing heavily. She counted to ten carefully before speaking.

"What's your explanation?" she finally asked.

He shrugged and went on eating. Ellen knocked the cereal bowl out of his hands and across the room. It shattered against the wall. Jeff stared at her, his blue eyes angry slits.

"What the hell did you do that for?" he yelled.

Ellen itched to slap him "Don't you ever swear at me again, do you understand?" she hissed.

He looked a little frightened. "OK. Sorry. Don't have a cow about it."

Ellen stood looking at the boy she had thought she knew. He still had a gangly look to him. His blue eyes still looked innocent.

"Jeff, your father and I have taught you morals. We have taught you to wait until marriage . . ." her voice trailed off.

He smirked. "Fat lot of good it does to wait. It didn't make you and Dad happy."

Ellen drew a deep breath. "This is not about your father and me. This is about you. Jeff, you are only fifteen. Megan is fourteen. Do you want to mess up the rest of your life?"

He stood up, his eyes blazing. "And who are *you* to preach at me? You and Dad have completely screwed up your lives. Yet you stand in front of me and tell *me* what to do?"

"I am still your mother," Ellen retorted angrily.

Jeff laughed. "Yeah, I know. You've made it perfectly clear. All my life it's been 'don't do this' and 'don't do that.' I never knew why. Do you remember what you said when I asked why?"

"No, and that do—"

He interrupted her. "You told me I had to behave because I was the pastor's son." He mimicked her high-pitched voice. "Jeffy, dear, you can't listen to that CD. What will people think? Jeffy, dear, you have to go to church every week because you're the pastor's son." He dropped his voice back to normal. "And all my life I knew you didn't really believe anything you taught me."

Ellen gasped. "I believe. Of course I believed it."

"Yeah, right. Then why did it make you so tight and judgmental all the time?" His voice rose. "I don't want your life. I don't want your church. I don't want your God. I want to live how I want to live. Like Dad does."

"As long as you're in this house, you will live by my rules, young man," Ellen countered angrily. "What your father does is between him and God."

Jeff turned to walk out of the kitchen, and Ellen grabbed his arm.

"You'll not walk out on me in the middle of a conversation," Ellen yelled.

He looked at her. "Why can't you mellow out a bit? Why can't you be like Sandy? She's cool. She never gets on my case about anything."

Ellen slapped him. A look of astonishment crossed Jeff's face, and she knew it mirrored her own. She had never slapped him before. An angry red mark appeared on his left cheek. She tried to hug him.

"Jeff, I'm sorry, I'm sorry," she whispered.

He still stared at her. Slowly, tears filled his eyes. His chin wobbled, but he straightened his back defiantly and shook her off.

"You want to know why Dad left you?" Jeff spat the words at her. "He left because you're too uptight and too picky. Sandy accepts people where they're at. You always want them to change."

Ellen felt wooden and lifeless. Drawing herself up straight, she prayed her voice wouldn't break.

"Jeff, these are the rules. Number one, no girls in the house. Period. Number two, if you get a girl pregnant, I will personally make sure you have to support the girl and the baby for the rest of their lives. Number three, do not ever, *ever*, mention that woman in this house again."

She turned and walked back to the bedroom, not trusting herself any further. She sat on the edge of the bed and stared out the bedroom window, feeling too shaken to cry. She got up and paced, then sat back down again. She wished she could go to sleep and never wake up again. Jeff slammed his bedroom door; then all went silent. Ellen sat, then paced. Paced, then sat. The hours slid by almost unnoticed. Outside the window, darkness gave way to a beautiful sunrise. She barely saw it. At six-thirty she dialed Frank's home number.

"Hello?" A sleepy answer.

She gripped the phone, imagining him lying in bed next to Sandy. "We need to talk."

He groaned. "Ellen, it's six-thirty in the morning. Can't this wait?"

"No. It's about Jeff."

He groaned. "OK, just a minute. Let me go to the other phone."

He doesn't want to disturb his precious Sandy, Ellen thought bitterly. She imagined Sandy without makeup and hoped she looked terrible.

"Hello. I'm back."

"I caught Jeff in bed with a girl last night."

"For Pete's sake, he's only fifteen!" Frank sounded awake

now—and worried.

"Yeah, well, I guess he learns quickly from his father." Ellen couldn't resist the dig.

"Ellen, if you're just going to insult me, I'll hang up." He sounded righteously indignant. Ellen wondered what he had to be indignant about.

She said nothing.

"Well, let me think about this," Frank finally said.

"He's not taking this well, Frank. He's getting worse and worse at home." Ellen gripped the phone as if to pull Frank closer.

"Let me think about it. I'll call you right back, OK?"

"OK." Ellen hung up the phone and stared out the window again. She listened for sounds of Jeff moving around, but the house was silent. Too silent. She shivered, feeling slightly ill.

Frank called back a judicious while later. Ellen was touched, thinking he'd given the problem lots of thought. But it seemed he had spent the time discussing Jeff with Sandy.

"Sandy says," he said authoritatively, "that Jeff should spend the summer with your parents or with mine. Maybe getting away would do him some good. She says it might be good for you too."

"Tell Sandy I truly appreciate her concern," Ellen snapped sarcastically.

Frank sounded hurt. "She was very sympathetic with you. She started to cry."

"Tell her thanks a lot for her sympathy. Why doesn't she show it by letting you come back?"

"I don't want to come back," Frank said, his voice grave and paternal.

"Fine, I don't want you either!" Ellen said, and hung up on him. She wondered at her sensation of joy, of release, then realized that in her anger with Frank, she had for the first time in hours thought of something other than Jeff and his problems.

Frank called back two hours later. Jeff had already grabbed his windsurf board and headed for the river.

"We'll send him to my parents in Seattle," he decreed.

Ellen sighed. "When?"

"I'll drive him up there this evening. Mom says they'll be glad to have him for an entire summer."

"He won't be happy about this."

"It's the best thing." Frank sounded authoritative and confident. *His pastor's voice,* Ellen thought idly.

"I wish he could go to Florida and stay with my parents," Ellen said. She worried that Frank's parents would poison Jeff against her.

"Do you want to pay the plane ticket?"

Ellen sighed. "No."

"Then I guess it's Seattle."

"Yeah."

Silence. "I'll be by this afternoon about four to pick him up. Make sure he's packed."

"OK. 'Bye."

First Frank. Now Jeff. Ellen knew she'd failed. She couldn't keep her husband, and now she couldn't be a good mother to her son. She felt her whole life was being stripped from her, layer by painful layer.

Jeff's words came back—you're too rigid; you want to change people. She pushed them away. She didn't want to examine and didn't want to think.

Frank showed up precisely at four. Jeff sat sullenly in the living room, his bags piled around him. He threw her accusing looks every time she walked into the room. Ellen ached to hold him, tell him she was sorry, but Jeff wouldn't let her near him. The weight of her guilt felt crushing.

Frank bustled to pack the car, a show of efficiency and

dutifulness. Ellen suddenly wondered if Sandy wanted Jeff to leave for the summer so she could have Frank to herself. The house that had seemed so big and empty without Frank now shrank around him and felt claustrophobic. Before, he had been in the house like air they unthinkingly breathed; now he showed his energy and duty like a display of the treasure they had wasted.

"You'll have a wonderful time in Seattle," she reassured Jeff.

He just looked at her, his silence filling her with guilt. *You're a terrible mother*, a voice screamed inside her. *You're a failure. You're a nobody. You can't even take care of your own son.*

Frank jingled his keys. "Well, we'd better hit the road."

Ellen hugged Jeff. He stood stiffly and didn't return her hug. Then Frank and Jeff climbed into the car. Ellen watched as the car backed slowly out of the driveway. She turned and walked back into the house. Its big emptiness terrified her. The weekend days and the week evenings stretched in front of her, empty and awful.

As Jeff's accusations came back, she buried her face in her hands. "I won't think about it," she whispered. "I will be strong."

She remembered the books she'd been reading. They all told the woman to be strong, to stand up for herself. Ellen buoyed herself by repeating some of the memorized words.

"I will be strong," she whispered. "I will take care of myself. I will be strong."

Outside, an eight-year-old neighbor boy skateboarding up the street brought back memories of Jeff, and Ellen blinked back tears.

"This is the best thing for him," she told herself sternly. "I will be strong. I will be strong."

Somehow, inside, she hoped she'd believe it.

Chapter 8

The divorce became final in July. The night after Ellen signed the papers, Katherine took her out for dinner.

"You're a free woman now," she said gaily. "Doesn't it feel great?"

Ellen tried to smile and say Yes. Instead of great, she felt dead inside, and the fettuccine tasted like mud. "At least I got the house," she mumbled.

"That's the best thing, really," Katherine assured her. "With the way real estate is going nuts in the gorge, you'll make a killing when you go to sell."

Ellen nodded. She tried to imagine selling the house, starting over. "He's not sending any alimony. Because I'm working, I'll get only child support."

Katherine sighed. "How did he get away with that?"

"I didn't fight him," Ellen admitted.

A waitress came up. "Can I get you anything else?"

"No, thank you," they both replied.

Katherine shook her head. "Why didn't you fight him?"

Ellen blinked back tears. "Because I thought if I were nice . . ." her voice trailed off.

Katherine finished the sentence. "You thought if you were nice, he might come back, right?"

Ellen nodded. "Pretty stupid, huh?" she said bitterly.

Katherine shook her head sympathetically. "I did the same thing."

Murmured conversations underscored the light background music. The food smelled delicious, but Ellen couldn't eat it.

"I'm going to have to get another job or something. I can't make the house payments on what I'm making." She looked at Katherine, suddenly embarrassed. "I'm not asking for a raise," she assured her.

"Why not give yourself a raise?" Katherine suggested.

"Huh?"

"Get your license. Sell insurance. Maybe you can set up your own office in Park Rapids. Our company doesn't have an office there. I've been expected to handle both Park Rapids and Riverhurst. There's too much business."

Ellen laughed. "It sounds great, but I don't think I'm good at sales."

"Yes you are."

"Why do you think so?"

"Because you don't give up easily. You know how to talk to people who come into the office." Katherine smiled at her. "Look, think about it. There's a two-week training and crash course in Portland the end of August. If you can come up with the money for the course, I'll give you the two weeks off with pay."

"Really?" Ellen stared at her.

"I want you making triple your ex's salary."

Ellen laughed. "That sounds wonderful."

"You'll do it in a year," Katherine promised.

Making that much money sounded too good to be possible. "I'll think about it," Ellen promised.

"Good. Would you like dessert?"

Ellen felt buoyant for the rest of the evening. When she drove home, she looked at the house and decided Mom's redecorating suggestions had been right. It needed a change.

She flicked on all the lights and the radio and started moving furniture around.

"Maybe I'll even sell the place," she said as she shoved the sofa under the window. She imagined buying one of the trendy new condos in Park Rapids and going into her own office every morning. And she'd be rich. Very, very rich.

She moved the chair across the room, then started taking books out of the bookcase. She piled them on the floor by the fireplace.

"I really should get rid of some of these," she muttered as she blew dust off the tops of a few books.

The picture albums came down next. She stacked them carefully on the floor, but they seemed to beckon her. Almost against her will, she plunked down on a cushion and opened the first one.

Memories tumbled out of it. Smiling pictures of her courtship with Frank. He looked young and scruffy with long hair and sideburns. She looked vulnerable in a short skirt and chunky shoes, her hair straight and long and parted in the middle. Ellen smiled, thinking the seventies had definitely been the worst fashion decade of the twentieth century.

She turned each page as if seeing the pictures for the first time. She looked at the faces. *Did we look happy? Were we ever really happy?* As she got to pictures of Jeff as a baby, she began to cry. She looked so proud, holding him at the Grand Canyon. Ellen remembered they'd taken a family vacation around the States that year.

She turned the pages, her tears flowing unchecked. Frank's hair began thinning; her hips began widening. The smiles on the faces became increasingly strained. They stood farther and farther apart for pictures. And Ellen knew, suddenly, that Sandy was a symptom rather than the cause of their destroyed marriage.

"But we could have worked it out," she whispered,

looking at the last pictures in the last album. "If you'd only given me a chance," she whispered to Frank's picture.

Where do I go from here? she wondered. She remembered the times she tried to get Frank back. She thought of his apparent happiness with Sandy.

I'm nearly forty. Who's going to want me?

She tried to imagine falling in love with prince charming and riding off into the sunset of eternal bliss. With a cynical laugh, Ellen vowed she'd never trust anyone again.

She looked around the living room, now rearranged but still the same. *I need a fresh start*, she decided. *I've got to sell the house.* She felt cold and bleak inside. *But it's the only thing I have left*, she argued. *It's the only connection with my entire past. Will I be me without the house? Who's "me" anyway?*

She thought of the hefty mortgage payments and her measly salary. Frank had said he'd be willing to sell the place for her in exchange for part of the profits.

"Fat chance," she muttered.

She stood up and slowly walked to the kitchen table. Pulling out her to-do list, she wrote "get an agent" on her list. She vowed she'd go to Frank's competitors.

Tired from moving furniture, Ellen got ready for bed and tried to sleep. The house felt so big and empty. The bed felt so big and empty. Ellen imagined Frank with Sandy. She fervently hoped he snored as loudly with her. But as she hugged the extra pillow tightly, she knew she would trade anything to hear him snore again.

Ellen put the house up for sale the next day. She told Katherine she wanted to go to the insurance training, and she started sorting through all her belongings. She allowed herself to think about the pain only at night.

"I'm a professional," she told herself. "I don't let my personal life interfere with my professional life."

The crying spells she had had for the first few months

after Frank left seemed to have dried up. The anger she now felt spurred her into a flurry of activity.

The house sold at the end of the month, and Ellen put the money into a tiny two-bedroom condo in Park Rapids. She wrote to Jeff, telling about the move and assuring him he'd still have a bedroom in the new place. She didn't expect a reply—he'd ignored her letters all summer—so when she got one a week later, she tore it open eagerly.

Dear Mom,

Congrats on selling the house. I think it's the best thing. I always liked Park Rapids better anyway. Better wind-surfing.

Grandma and Grandpa want me to go to the Christian boarding school up here by Seattle. I've written and told Dad about it too. I think it would be cool. My friends from up here are going there this fall.

I'm really sorry about what I said the night before I left. Grandma told me it wasn't fair to compare you to, well, you know who.

Anyway, catch you later.

Love, Jeff

Ellen folded the letter and chewed her bottom lip. She had just assumed Jeff would be going away to boarding school that fall, but hadn't thought about where. And she hadn't thought about where the money would come from.

The money. When Frank had worked for the church, the church paid for a large portion of Jeff's tuition. Ellen thought of the hefty private-school bill and knew she couldn't pay it. She called Frank.

"Did you hear from Jeff?" she asked.

"Yeah. Wants to go to boarding school." A sigh. "I can't send him."

Ellen felt a headache starting. "I can't either." She

thought a minute. "What are we going to do?"

"Let me see what I can come up with. I'll call back."

Ellen hung up and stared out the window of her new living room. It didn't have much of a view, and the neighbor's stereo seemed to be on twenty-four hours a day. But at least the payments were lower than the house payments.

She wondered at her casual conversation with Frank. She didn't feel anything talking to him. Nothing. She thought of all the books she'd read outlining the pain of divorce and felt proud. She could handle it. She was bigger than it.

I'm over him, she thought, smiling.

She didn't ask herself why she didn't feel anything in any area of her life. She didn't question why all food tasted bland or why she woke up each morning with a stress headache.

Frank called back two hours later. "My parents will pay for Jeff's schooling, if that's OK with you," he informed her.

"Great. Fine. Tell them thank you."

"It's the least they can do after raising a son like Frank," she muttered as she hung up.

Three days later, Ellen enrolled in the insurance training course. Two weeks before leaving for the seminar, she had run into Pat in the grocery store.

"Ellen! How are you?" Pat asked, nudging her cart closer.

Ellen groaned inwardly. *Didn't Pat get the message when I never came back to church?* "Doing great, thank you."

"Are you living in Park Rapids now?" Pat asked.

"Yes." Ellen hoped if she kept her answers short, the woman would go away. Seeing people from her past made her feel bleak and empty. She wanted to get away as fast as she could.

"We'd love to see you in church," Pat pressed.

"Ah . . . well . . . thank you." Ellen looked helplessly around for an escape.

Pat opened her purse and wrote quickly on a slip of paper. She handed the paper to Ellen with a smile.

"This is my phone number. I'm here if you ever want to talk."

Ellen felt a flash of anger. "I'm doing fine, Pat. Really." *Do I look like a victim?* Ellen wondered.

Pat smiled. "I'm so glad to hear it. I'll be praying for you."

Ellen thanked her and escaped around the corner with her cart. She angrily pulled groceries from the shelves and threw them into the basket. *How dare she presume!* she thought, her face flaming.

Ellen realized she hadn't thought much about the church since her mother had returned to Florida. And she knew she didn't want to start thinking about the church now. She stuffed the scrap of paper into her purse and told herself to throw it away when she got home.

I've got to maintain control, she told herself as she loaded the groceries into the back of the van. *I've got to keep going.*

She drove fast all the way home, hoping to escape the bleak feeling that seeing Pat had given her. She rolled down the windows and let the hot summer air blow her hair to disarray. She felt frantic inside and nervous.

I will maintain control, Ellen told herself again.

By the time she got home, she almost believed it. As she put food away, she laughed at her earlier anxiety.

I don't need the church; I don't need anyone, she told herself.

Outside, the sun beckoned. Ellen poured herself a cold soda, put on a pair of shorts, and sat out on her deck to read a magazine. But the glossy articles failed to hold her attention. Her thoughts kept drifting back to Pat. Finally, irritated, she closed the magazine and shut her eyes. Images came back. She remembered Pat's abrupt divorce from her husband. Then, three years later, her son dying of AIDS. The official story was that he contracted it through intravenous drug use. No one knew for sure. Ellen shuddered.

"Why can't she just leave me alone?" she muttered.

It made her paranoid. Maybe Pat could see something she couldn't. Ellen shook her head and opened her eyes. In the distance she could hear children splashing in the condominium pool. She picked up the magazine and started to read again. An article caught her attention—"How to Add Spice to Your Marriage." Ellen flipped past it quickly.

She thought of Jeff's going away to school and worried for him. *How would he adjust? Would the other kids know what had happened to his parents and ostracize him? Would he want to come home again? Would he get mixed up in drugs?* She thought of Pat's son and shuddered again. He'd died a horrible death. Pneumonia. She dutifully went to visit him during his last week. He'd been unconscious. Ellen remembered being afraid to touch him. The nurses had apparently felt the same because he looked dirty and unkempt.

Ellen sighed and tried again to focus on the magazine. *That's Pat's problem, not mine*, she reminded herself. *Besides, there's nothing I can do about it now anyway.*

Turning the page, she found an interesting article on home decoration and started reading.

Chapter 9

Ellen felt him staring at her again. She sneaked a look across the rows of tables to where he sat taking notes. He saw her, blushed, and looked away. Ellen blushed too and quickly looked back at the instructor.

". . . when you want to show the customer the difference between whole and term life insurance . . ."

Ellen tried to listen, but her thoughts kept returning to Bill, sitting five people down from her. Insurance training. A group of middle-aged adults trying to make career switches midlife filled the room. In the back, a few recent college graduates sat with their new briefcases and sharp suits. She stared at her class notes and scribbled the date absently across the top of the page. August 23. *I'm forty years old today*, she thought, not for the first time.

She remembered her thirty-ninth birthday. Frank had brought home a silk scarf and a brooch. Ellen hadn't liked either—they seemed too flashy and not her style. Now, after meeting Sandy, Ellen realized whose style they were. *This year's sure different*, she thought as she automatically wrote down the instructor's words. She had never once imagined she'd be sitting here, in Portland, exactly a year later. She thought life would go on the same, year after year, forever.

She remembered her first birthday they had celebrated

together as a married couple. Ellen had turned twenty-two. Frank had scraped together enough money to buy her the skirt she'd been longing for. As she sat staring at the page, she wondered whatever had happened to that skirt.

Insurance training. Is this what I really want to be doing? Ellen suddenly thought. *Triple my ex-husband's salary,* she reminded herself. *It sounds like a hollow goal,* she admitted. *But it's all I've got left.* She devoted her full attention to the instructor again.

Bill caught up with her as the session ended. He stood nervously nearby while she bent over the drinking fountain.

"Those sessions sure are long," he said as she straightened.

Ellen smiled. "Yeah. A two-week course didn't sound half bad a month ago!"

Bill smoothed his salt-and-pepper hair and grinned at her. Ellen liked the way his clean-shaven face crinkled when he smiled. She looked away quickly.

"Ah . . . would you like to have dinner with me tonight?" Bill asked haltingly.

Ellen glanced at him, and a ruddy red crept up his neck.

"Um . . . I don't know . . ." She wanted to say Yes and relieve his embarrassment, but she felt panicked at the thought of going on a date. A date! She hadn't dated for almost twenty years.

"Well, we could talk about insurance, maybe help each other study." He looked at her hopefully.

A shrill yapping from across the hotel lobby distracted them. Ellen whirled around just in time to see a toy poodle, complete with the jeweled collar, straining against its leash that had apparently been caught in the elevator door. She watched, horrified, as the dog slid up the side of the closed elevator, its yipping becoming frantic. Hotel personnel rushed to the rescue and unhooked the dog's collar just before it disappeared between the elevator and the top of the door.

". . . told Mother she was getting forgetful. Now look what she almost did to that dog. . . ." A disgruntled man stalked by, talking to a middle-aged woman by his side.

Ellen lowered her eyes quickly and tried not to laugh. Now that the dog's safety was ensured, the situation struck her as funny. She sneaked a look at Bill. The corners of his mouth twitched.

Ellen lost all semblance of control and burst into laughter. Bill joined her. Other people gave them censoring stares, but that only made them laugh harder.

"When that dog started levitating up the elevator . . ." Ellen tried to talk but couldn't. Tears ran down her cheeks. She leaned against Bill, and he automatically reached out and supported her with his arm.

Their laughter died, and Ellen felt awkward with Bill's arm around her. He dropped it quickly. The laughter seemed to remove her earlier fear.

"I'd love to go to dinner with you," Ellen told him warmly. "Shall I meet you in the hotel restaurant about seven?"

He looked surprised. "Seven would be perfect."

Ellen looked at her watch. "Oops, break is almost up. We'd better get back in there."

When they returned to the conference room, Bill moved to a chair beside Ellen. Neither said anything as the instructor started lecturing again.

She met him outside the restaurant at five minutes after seven. She'd prepared carefully—choosing her favorite red dress and doing her hair and makeup artfully. She felt nervous. He stood, wearing a suit and tie, and clenching and unclenching his hands. She felt sorry for him, knowing he was probably as nervous as she. He smiled at her as she walked up, and she could tell he liked the way she looked but felt too shy to say anything. The headwaiter led them to a table in the back.

Ellen looked around the restaurant and admired the soft lighting and muted music. She recognized several people from the insurance training course and smiled at them. They looked at Bill, then at her and pretended not to notice. Ellen flushed hotly. She slid into the chair the headwaiter held out for her. Bill settled into the chair opposite her.

Bill smiled across the table at her. "I thought you were going to turn me down. All evening I kept expecting you to call and say you'd changed your mind."

Ellen shrugged. "I was going to," she said honestly. "But today's my fortieth birthday, and I decided I didn't want to spend it alone with room service and TV."

"Your birthday? I'm honored." He waved the waiter over. "Let me buy you a drink. How about champagne?"

Ellen blushed. "I don't drink. Maybe a Martinelli's or a virgin piña colada?"

Bill ordered two virgin piña coladas, then turned back to her. "So, tell me about yourself. Where are you from? What did you do before insurance? Are you married? Do you have kids?"

Ellen laughed and held up her hands. "Whoa! One at a time!" She thought a minute. "Well, right now I'm living in Park Rapids, but I'm originally from Minnesota. Before insurance I was a pastor's wife. I am divorced, and I have a fifteen-year-old son." She felt amazed she could say this without any trace of emotion. "What about you?"

"I'm from Eugene, and I used to work in the timber industry, but you know what's going on with *that*." He grimaced. "Anyway, I'm divorced, and I don't have any kids. I'm a born-again Christian."

Oh, no. Ellen winced, feeling an emptiness inside. *Here comes the great conversion story. He'll tell me how God lifted him out of drug addiction and social despair and put him on the path of true, middle-class, conservative churchism. What about when God takes you out of that true path and dumps you back into despair?* Ellen wondered bitterly.

"It's exciting to meet other Christians, isn't it?" Bill continued. "It doesn't happen very often."

Ellen nodded and pretended interest in her menu. She couldn't read the words. The menu shook in front of her. *How did he know? Was it because I didn't order champagne? Was it because I used to be married to a pastor? Do all those years of working in the church show on me? I could be an atheist for all he knows!*

The thought amused her. Not believing in God wasn't an option. If God didn't exist, whom could she blame? At whom, besides Frank and that woman, could she funnel her anger?

The waiter came back, bearing their drinks. Ellen sipped hers while he stood and waited for their order.

"I'll take the pasta primavera," she finally said, closing the menu. She regretted the choice almost instantly. It would take too long to eat. She wanted something fast so she could escape and get back to her room. She wondered why she had agreed to the dinner. *If I'd known he'd preach at me, I'd never have said Yes*, she thought.

Bill ordered a steak, and the waiter whisked their menus away. Ellen smiled mechanically at him.

"So how did you become a Christian?" Bill asked.

He doesn't let things drop, does he? "I was raised a Christian," Ellen replied, her voice flat.

"I met Christ shortly after my divorce," Bill said. "When my wife left, I wanted to die. I drank too much, trying to escape. That lasted for about a year until I walked past a church one evening, heard singing inside, and decided to slip into the back." He smiled, his eyes focused on the table lamp. "I just kept coming back to that church, and I gave my life to God. He helped me turn my life around, get my drinking under control, and even forgive my ex-wife."

"That's nice," Ellen commented, tapping one foot impatiently under the table. *Frank gets forgiveness from me when you-know-what freezes over*, she wanted to add.

"How long have you and your husband been separated?" Bill asked.

"Seven months. Eight. I don't know." She smiled woodenly at the waiter as he placed their plates in front of them.

"You're doing so well. I wish I'd known Christ when Roberta left." He speared his steak and slicked off a small portion.

Ellen knew he wanted to know what happened with Frank, but she didn't think it was any of his business. She twirled the pasta sharply, splattering a little cream on the table. She slowed the twirl a bit, telling herself to maintain control.

"So, what do you think of the training course so far?" she asked brightly, changing the subject.

He looked a little hurt. "It's good. I suppose we'll find out when we sit for our exams at the end, huh?"

Ellen nodded. She tried to think of something to say, but the cold feeling inside made everything seem useless. She wanted to escape to her room, turn on the TV, and turn off her mind. She'd discovered soon after Frank left that too much thinking did more harm than good.

"I hope to open an office in Park Rapids as soon as I can," Ellen said. "My boss—Katherine—says she'll help me get started."

Bill studied her as she spoke. She knew she smiled a little too much and laughed a little too loud, but couldn't seem to stop herself. He looked disappointed. Ellen wanted to tell him she didn't owe him a discussion about God, her personal life, or anything else.

They discussed insurance for the rest of the meal. Ellen

declined dessert, feigned exhaustion, and escaped to her room. Bill walked her to her door.

"I'm sorry if I got too personal back there," he said as they stepped off the elevator. "I'm not very good at this dating thing yet. I haven't gone out with anyone since I became a Christian."

"No, it was fine," Ellen lied, trying to make him feel better.

He looked hopeful. "Really? I was just so excited to meet another Christian . . ."

Ellen turned to unlock her door. "Well, thank you. I'll see you tomorrow in class."

He bent and kissed her cheek softly. "Thank *you*. You are a classy lady, and I had a wonderful evening." He turned and walked back onto the elevator, leaving Ellen speechless.

She opened her door automatically, closed it behind her, then leaned against it. She could still feel his kiss. She smiled and kicked her shoes off. Suddenly she felt young, beautiful, and terribly glamorous.

"What is it they say about life beginning at forty?" she asked aloud.

She walked across the room, unzipping her dress as she walked. *Bill's a really nice guy*, she reasoned. *But a Christian.* She shuddered. Frank had been just as sincere, just as enthusiastic. She wondered how long it would be before Bill showed his true self.

She stopped in front of the window and looked at the lights of Portland. They were just coming on in the late-evening dusk, and there seemed to be millions. She leaned her forehead against the cool glass and closed her eyes.

"Happy birthday to me," she whispered.

She turned from the window, finished undressing, and climbed into bed. It was too early to sleep, so she lay and watched the rest of the day die away and the city lights sparkle. She kept thinking of Bill's comments about Christianity. It seemed to have worked for him. *It won't forever*, Ellen thought bitterly. *If the church people don't get him, God will.* She wondered at her bitterness. A year ago she would have called a person like herself a heretic and a sinner.

Well, add that to my list of sins, she muttered, and wrapped the sheet closer around her.

Ellen admitted to herself that she envied Bill. She badly wanted to return to that easy Christian belief and trust. *But it doesn't work*, she wanted to scream. *It's not real. Working hard is real. Trying to do what you can is real. Nothing else is. God doesn't care.* Deep inside she hoped she was wrong.

Chapter 10

Ellen left the training seminar with passing scores on all her exams and with Bill's address and phone number—and arrived home just in time to help Jeff pack for academy. After two days of whirlwind packing and supply buying, she drove him to the campus and said a tearful goodbye. He seemed anxious to see her drive away.

She started selling insurance the week after she got her license. It seemed easy. She sold two health-insurance packages her first week out and impressed Katherine.

"If you keep going like this, you'll have your own office by next year," Katherine predicted.

Bill wrote letters about his progress selling in Eugene. He didn't mention Christianity again, which relieved Ellen. She faithfully returned his letters, keeping her replies chatty and impersonal.

"So, who is this guy?" Katherine teased.

Ellen blushed. "Just someone I met at the training seminar," she said defensively.

"Sounds heavy. Did you sleep with him?"

Ellen threw a paper wad at her. "Of course not! How could you even think such a thing?"

Katherine shrugged. "I thought you'd want to get revenge."

Ellen shook her head. "Not that way." Since Frank's betrayal, sex held no interest for her.

September sped by. Ellen sent a huge gift up to Jeff for his sixteenth birthday. He sounded proud and important on the phone when she talked to him. He wanted to get his driver's license, and Ellen shuddered as she ran the numbers on what insurance would cost her. She told him he'd have to wait until Christmas vacation.

She continued selling. She splurged on her first commission check and bought herself an expensive wool suit and a pair of plush leather pumps. She bought a soft briefcase to complete the outfit.

October arrived—raining, cold, and miserable. Frank called late one evening, and Ellen picked up the phone just as she came in the door.

"Where were you? I've been trying to reach you all evening!" His strident voiced seemed to leap out of the phone.

"I was out on a hot date. What business is it of yours?"

A pause. "Really?"

Ellen considered telling him the truth, but decided against it. *Let him wonder*, she decided. "What do you want?"

"Well, I wanted to talk with you."

Ellen sighed and dropped into a chair. "Look, it's been a long day. Why don't you call me tomorrow?"

"Well, I really wanted to talk now. I have some news. Sandy and I are getting married."

Ellen dropped the phone.

"Ellen? Ellen, are you there?"

She picked up the receiver woodenly. "That's nice. Congratulations."

"Well, I just thought you should know. We're driving to Reno this weekend."

"Sounds just Sandy's style," Ellen muttered. "I suppose

she has former 'business associates' down there."

"Huh?"

"One-nine-hundred hire a whore," Ellen spat back.

Frank hung up on her with a muffled curse. She slammed the phone down and glared at it, angry tears forming.

"I hate you, I hate you, I hate you," she screamed.

The people next door banged on the wall to quiet her down. Ellen ripped the phone out of its socket and threw it across the room. It landed in the corner with a thud and muffled ring.

"He doesn't deserve to be happy," she cried. "He should be miserable and alone!"

She sobbed as she remembered reading that older women had a better chance of being taken hostage by terrorists than getting married. Or was it being shot by terrorists? It didn't matter.

Who's going to want me? She tried to think of anyone her age who had remarried but realized she didn't know of anyone. Even Katherine—for all her success—had never met anyone.

She tried to stop crying. The tears fell harder. All the pain she thought she'd successfully buried came rushing back, and she curled up on the floor, unable to move. She imagined Frank saying those vows to another woman— love forever, forsaking all others—and she remembered their wedding nearly eighteen years before.

Soft, flowing white dress. Flowers in her hair. A January wedding. Wedding music accompanied by a guitar. It looked so different from her parents' formal church wedding of years before, but the vows were the same. Love, honor, and cherish. Forsake all others. In sickness and in health.

Ellen stayed curled up on the floor, not caring that her suit was getting wrinkled. Her tears slowly stopped, but she couldn't summon the energy to move. She began to shiver uncontrollably and knew the chill came from within.

The alarm woke her hours later. She groggily sat up and found herself still on the floor and still wearing her suit. Stumbling to the bedroom, she turned off the clock. Ellen briefly considered calling in sick, but didn't want to spend the day alone.

What does it matter if I go to work or stay home? she wondered as she stepped into the shower. *What does it matter if I do anything?*

She remembered hearing about people dying in their homes and not being found for weeks because they had no one close to them who cared. *Would that happen to me if I died?*

She leaned against the shower wall and slowly lathered her hair. Everything felt like slow motion. She wasn't surprised to see, when she stepped out of the shower, that she had taken twice as long as usual.

Ellen skipped breakfast. The thought of food made her nauseated. She drove distractedly to work, nearly sideswiping another car. Once there, she typed four errors in one of Katherine's letters.

"Ellen, is everything all right?" Katherine asked.

Ellen nodded. "Fine. Why?"

Katherine handed her the letter, errors circled. "You usually catch your mistakes."

Ellen shrugged. "I'll fix them."

She brought the letter back up on the computer and corrected the errors quickly. *Anyone can do this*, Ellen thought. *If I'm not here, will it really matter? Katherine will find another divorcée to befriend. I could disappear, and nobody would know the difference.*

As the day dragged by, Ellen frequently found herself staring at blank walls, unable to concentrate on her work. Flashbacks of her life with Frank kept interrupting her. The memories came back so sharply that the pain left her breathless. She kept trying to rewrite the past and the present.

It's all been a bad dream. I'll go home to my old house, and Frank will be there. Or, he and Sandy will be in an accident, and Sandy will be killed. Or he'll leave her.

She finished her work early and left the office. *Why should I try to sell anything? It won't matter anyway. No one will buy.* She drove home and sat unseeing in front of the TV. She finally turned the sound off and just stared at the pictures. When the stations went off the air, she tried to sleep.

She called in sick the next day. And the day after that. After several days, Katherine started to sound irritated. Ellen couldn't explain. She couldn't get out of her bathrobe. The food in the house dwindled to nearly nothing. Rather than buy groceries, Ellen stopped eating.

Why, God? Why? She cried it constantly.

She barely slept. But when she did, the dreams made her cry. She dreamed she was free, happy, in love with Frank. They were on vacation together. Jeff was still a baby. She woke sobbing.

She wanted to smooth Frank's hair one more time and tell him the thinning wasn't really noticeable. She longed to curl up in his lap and feel his arms wrapped around her. She realized that, other than hugging Jeff, she hadn't touched anyone since Frank had left. She ached to hug someone. And she now understood why Katherine had affairs. The touching, even more than the sex, was what she physically missed the most.

"Would anyone care if I disappeared?" She whispered the words to herself, savoring the possibilities. *If God doesn't care, and the church doesn't care, and my husband—whom I pledged my life to—doesn't care, and my son is away and probably won't care, who's left? I don't love my job enough to live for it.*

She saw herself growing old and bitter. Wrinkles would appear, her hair would gray, she'd keep birds and tacky ceramic pieces. She'd be mean and crotchety and scare all the children in the neighborhood.

What's Katherine's future? she wondered. *What will she do when she's too old to attract men? Will her business keep her warm? Or will she just live in a big house and have wrinkles, gray hair, birds, and ceramics?*

The ache that started when Frank phoned didn't diminish. It went deeper. The weekend arrived, and Ellen still sat staring at the walls.

God, if You love me, You'll work things out. You'll make me feel better. Silence. No reply.

She remembered an Edgar Allen Poe short story she'd read in college titled "The Maelstrom." As she thought of the swirling black water, she knew that's how she felt. Everything swirled faster and faster around her, while she got sucked in deeper and deeper. The light at the top of the whirlpool disappeared. And Ellen imagined she would see the pieces of her life swirling around her, broken and useless.

Would anyone care if I just disappeared?

Driven by hunger and desperation, Ellen dressed and walked to the nearest market. She was afraid to drive, afraid that if she got behind the wheel of the van, she'd purposefully drive it off the road. She'd always condemned suicide as a sin. Now it looked like a blessing.

The weekend went by in a fog. Ellen started staring at the living-room clock, just watching the second hand move around the face. She found she could do this for hours at a time and not feel bored.

She dragged herself back to work on Monday, afraid that if she didn't, Katherine would fire her. Katherine pulled Ellen into her office as soon as she walked in.

"Ellen, you have to pull yourself together," she said sternly. "Work is the only antidote."

Ellen felt guilty. "I'll be here. I promise."

Katherine sighed. "What happened? You were doing so well."

"I don't know," Ellen whispered. "Frank called to say he was getting married, and inside me something just snapped. I can't seem to do anything anymore. I just want to stare at the wall."

Katherine stared at her. "You need to see someone," she stated.

Ellen sighed. "No one can do any good."

Katherine reached for the phone book. "I'm serious. You need to see someone."

Ellen felt tears pushing at her eyes, and she blinked them back. *Does Katherine care? She just wants to make sure her work gets done right. No one cares.*

Ellen took the phone book from Katherine. "Maybe I'll call later."

Katherine handed her the phone. "Call someone *now*. I'll leave the room."

She got up and walked out, shutting the door behind her. Ellen sighed and flipped through the yellow pages to Counselors. After calling several, she found one who would take her that evening. She handed Katherine the phone book on her way out.

"I made an appointment for this evening," she told her sulkily.

Katherine touched her arm softly. "I've been there. I know. If you ever need to talk, call me."

Ellen smiled a tight smile. "Sure. Thanks."

Ellen wondered what she would tell the counselor. After work, she considered not showing for the appointment, but drove across town anyway. *It's better than sitting home staring at the walls,* she reasoned.

The counselor's waiting room looked understatedly elegant. But Ellen barely noticed the soft green carpet and cream furniture as she waited her turn. After a few minutes, the counselor came out and extended his hand.

"Hello. I'm Bob Cheeks. You must be Ellen."

Ellen shook his hand and hid a grin. With dimples and a baby-wide face, he'd been well-named, she decided. She followed him into his office, half expecting to see a psychiatrist couch. Instead, the small office held a desk and a seating area with three plush chairs. She sat down uncertainly in the nearest chair. Bob sat across from her.

"As I stated on the phone, I am a licensed marriage and family counselor. I deal with your problems here and now—not delving into past events unless it becomes apparent that those events are greatly disrupting your life now."

Ellen nodded, watching his mustache twitch as he spoke. He kept talking, but she tuned it out. *This is what Frank used to do*, she thought. *This is how he met Sandy.* She looked at the wedding ring on Bob's left hand and wondered if he had ever had an affair with one of his counselees. And she suddenly wondered if she shouldn't have chosen a woman counselor.

". . . do you have any questions?"

Ellen shook her head. "No. I'm here because a friend thought I should be." *I don't need you; I don't want your help*, she wanted to say.

He smoothed his mustache. "I see. What does you friend think is the problem?"

"She thinks I'm depressed since my divorce. But I'm not." Ellen nearly choked on the lie.

"Well, divorce is a traumatic event." He stopped encouragingly.

Ellen let the silence grow uncomfortable. She tapped a foot and didn't say anything.

He finally spoke. "What would you like to talk about, Ellen?"

She shrugged. "My divorce, I guess." She felt a rush of anger. *Who did this man think he was?* "My husband was a minister, and he left me for another woman after seventeen years of marriage. He's marrying her. There. Now you have it. If you can fix that, then I'm sure you're worth the money I'm paying you!" She glared at him defiantly.

"I'm not going to 'fix' anything. You are," he replied calmly.

Ellen stood up and grabbed her purse. "Then I don't need to pay you a hundred and ten an hour, do I?"

She strode out of the office and into her van. Her hands shook as she gripped the steering wheel. *I knew it was a bad idea; I knew it,* Ellen thought. *Just a quack, telling me to fix myself while he collects exorbitant fees!*

She braked to a stop in front of her condominium. *Fine. If he wants me to fix myself, I will. I don't need him. I don't need anyone.*

"I don't need anyone," she said out loud.

The words echoed off the walls, making the rooms feel cold and lonely.

"I can't keep going anymore," she whispered. "I can't."

Hugging herself, Ellen curled up on the sofa. She remembered a Bible promise she'd quoted to other people. God will not give us more than we can bear.

"God, this is more than I can bear. I can't go on. I'm sorry," she whispered.

She imagined getting up every day, trudging through her responsibilities, and collapsing at the end of the day. Why? What did it matter? The achy loneliness inside wouldn't go away. It wouldn't make Frank come back.

She realized that all the time she had thought she was over Frank, she just hadn't accepted that he was gone. Even when Ellen had signed the divorce papers, she thought he'd come back. That's the way it happened in the romances. Now, for the first time, his desertion felt real.

And Ellen knew she couldn't bear it.

The memories haunted her again. The way Frank used to wake her up on Sunday mornings with hugs and kisses. Or the way he read all the way through the paper in the morning before leaving for work. She could almost see him sitting with his legs stretched out in front of him, a silent frown on his face, as he read about world events.

I should have discussed world events with him more. I should have listened to him more. No wonder he left.

She remembered waking up in the middle of the night and reaching out to touch him. She remembered hearing his gentle snores and feeling secure, knowing he was beside her. The memories crumbled into ashes as she looked around the empty living room and listened to the dull thump of the neighbor's stereo.

Would anyone care if I disappeared?

No. And Ellen wondered how she could get up the next morning.

Chapter 11

October crawled by. Ellen slept little, ate little, and cared about nothing. She knew she looked terrible, but she didn't care. Every night, in bed, she imagined a gun pointed at her temple and her finger pulling the trigger. Thoughts of Frank brought nagging guilt. *I should have been a better wife. I should have done things differently.*

By the beginning of November, Ellen had decided on sleeping pills. The way to go would be sleeping pills. She came to this solution after eliminating other more gruesome ways of ending her life. At first she had considered a gun. But she didn't know how to buy one, much less load and fire one. Besides, she'd heard that gunshot wounds were very messy. What about driving the car off the road? She was afraid the crash might not be fatal, and she'd end up paralyzed instead. Razor blades? She'd heard that didn't work. Pills, then. She liked the idea of just going to sleep and never waking up.

Reaching a decision gave her strength, and she worked through the next couple weeks with her old energy. Katherine stopped watching her closely and started treating her like normal again. On Friday, a week before Thanksgiving, she finished all her work for the week and stayed late to start the next week's work.

"You're really back in the saddle, aren't you?" Katherine

commented as she left for the day. "Just be sure to lock up when you leave."

Ellen nodded and went on working. After she finished everything on her desk, she drove to all the grocery stores in town and bought one package of sleeping pills at each one. She figured buying several packages in one store might look suspicious. At the last store, she bought the strongest bottle of alcohol she could find. Vodka. She'd read mixing drugs and alcohol nearly always proved fatal.

Once home, she wrote letters to Katherine and Jeff and her parents. She figured Frank didn't deserve a letter. But nothing sounded right. In frustration, she tore the letters into little pieces. She took the pills out of their packages and piled them on the table. The vodka looked clear, like water.

"Can I do this?" she whispered.

She imagined a sad funeral, a nice burial—then eventually they'd all forget her. Jeff would be in therapy for the rest of his life, trying to understand his parents' divorce and his mother's suicide.

I'd better write him a letter, Ellen decided.

She tried again. "My dearest son. I know you don't understand why I did what I did, but I hope you will forgive me. Please live your life happily, fully. I'm sorry. Mom."

She started crying. *I want to see him grow up and get married. I want to see my grandchildren. But is it worth it?* She looked at the pile of pills gleaming temptingly. Taking a glass out of the cupboard, Ellen filled it to the brim with vodka and took a sip.

The burning sensation seemed to put her entire body on fire. She coughed violently, spilling vodka on herself. *How can people drink this stuff regularly?* She tried again. The burning was less intense this time.

She picked up a handful of pills and raised them to her mouth, then lowered them, too afraid to swallow them.

"Maybe I need a little Russian courage," she mumbled, and drank some more vodka.

She thought of the neighbors or Katherine finding her, rushing her to the hospital.

I should have done this somewhere else, she thought. It's not fair that someone has to find the body. *Why didn't I do this in an anonymous hotel room?* She decided to drive somewhere and take the pills.

As Ellen stood up, the room spun around. Walking slowly, drink in one hand, pills in the other, she careened through the house.

"I can't drive anywhere like this," she muttered. "I want to kill myself, not everyone else on the road."

She weaved to the bathroom and sat on the floor. The bright pills tantalized her, and she raised them to her mouth. But instead of swallowing them, Ellen lowered her hand and dumped the pills into the toilet. Stumbling back to the table, she gathered the rest of the pills and flushed them too.

You chicken, she raged at herself. *You can't even commit suicide properly!*

Between sobs, Ellen finished the glass of vodka and poured herself another. She was beginning to feel sick.

"I have to talk to someone," she cried out.

Opening her date book, she found Katherine's number and squinted at it. She picked up the receiver and tried to dial. The phone rang once. Twice.

"Hi, this is Katherine! I can't come to the phone—"

Ellen slammed down the receiver. The vodka felt alive in her stomach, and she began to wish she had taken the pills instead so she wouldn't feel so nauseated.

She dumped her purse upside down on the floor and pawed through the contents, looking for Bill's address and phone number. Her stomach lurched again, and she rushed to the bathroom, barely making it in time. And now her head started pounding.

Back in the living room, a scrap of paper caught her attention. She picked it up. Pat. Instinctively, Ellen picked up the phone and dialed Pat's number.

"Hello?"

"Hello. This is Ellen. . . ." She couldn't continue. She hung up and sobbed. *What am I doing? Why am I calling this woman?* The phone started ringing, and she ignored it. Finally, after ten rings, it stopped.

"You miserable coward," she hissed to herself. She wished she could get the pills back and take them. She wished she had the coordination to get to the car and drive it off a cliff somewhere. She pawed through the pile on the floor, this time looking for the van keys. Finding them at last, Ellen weaved to the bedroom and tried to put on a coat but kept missing the sleeve with her arm. She left it hanging and lurched back to the living room. A loud pounding on the door distracted her.

"Go away," she called, then held her head, wishing she hadn't said anything.

The pounding continued. Ellen staggered to the door, anxious to stop the noise. She opened it a crack. Pat stood on the doorstep.

"Ellen!" Pat pushed the door open and came into the living room.

Ellen followed, holding onto the wall as she walked. "It's nice of you to come over, but I'm really—"

Pat took her arm and led her to the sofa. "Did you take anything?" Her gray eyes looked like steel.

Ellen hung her head. "No. Just alcohol. Didn't have the nerve . . ."

Pat exhaled and relaxed against the sofa.

Ellen started crying again. "I just didn't want to wake up. I just wanted to go to sleep forever."

Pat wrapped her arms around Ellen and let her cry. Pat

held her quietly, not saying anything.

"I'm so embarrassed," Ellen finally mumbled against Pat's shoulder.

Pat drew back, holding her by her shoulders. "You reached out in time. You have no reason to be embarrassed."

Ellen flushed deep red. "Here I am, your former pastor's wife, drunk." She hiccuped with laughter.

Pat held her hand. "I've been there."

Ellen felt a rush of pain. "I just can't go on. I can't face anything anymore," she whispered.

Pat just listened.

"Every day I wake up and wish I were dead. Every night I go to sleep praying I won't wake up again. I feel I'm in the middle of a hurricane. It never lets up. I never get any peace. When I sleep, I dream. When I'm awake, I remember."

Pat nodded, but still didn't speak.

Ellen turned to her. "How did you do it? How did you keep going?"

"One foot in front of the other. God brought me through." Pat looked serious and very strong.

Ellen snorted. "God! He's the One who got me into this mess."

Pat opened her mouth to say something, then closed it again. "Are you seeing a counselor?" she asked.

"I had one session," Ellen admitted. "But I got angry and walked out."

Pat took Ellen's hands and looked deeply into her eyes. "I want you to promise me that you will go back to your counselor. You can't get through this alone. And you need to know that the person you're talking to is qualified to help you."

Ellen nodded, feeling very tired. "I don't think I can stay awake much longer."

Pat helped her off the sofa and led her to the bedroom. She turned down the covers and helped Ellen slide between the sheets. Ellen clutched her hand.

"Thank you," she whispered, before falling asleep.

She woke to the smell of eggs and hash browns. She sat up gingerly and was relieved to find her nausea gone and her headache dulled. Morning light filled the bedroom, and rain beat against the window. She rose slowly, put on a bathrobe, and shuffled to the kitchen. Pat stood over the stove, turning a fried egg.

"What are you doing here?" Ellen asked.

"I figured you'd be hungry." She pointed to the table. "Sit. It's almost ready."

Ellen obeyed. "Did you stay all night?" she asked as Pat put the food in front of her.

"I thought you might need me. The sofa is very comfortable." Pat put food on another plate and sat down across the table.

Ellen blinked back tears. "I—I don't know what to say. Why did you do this for me?"

Pat smiled gently. "Because you needed me. And I love you as a sister in Christ."

Ellen drew back, waiting for a sermon. It didn't materialize. Instead, Pat started eating the eggs with obvious relish. Ellen picked at hers. They looked delicious, but her stomach still felt a little weak. Ellen studied Pat. Short salt-and-pepper hair, gray eyes, an extra twenty pounds. She looked like an average middle-aged woman. But as Ellen sat looking at her, she thought Pat was one of the most beautiful people she'd ever seen.

Pat caught her staring and stopped eating. "Are you going to eat?" she asked, pointing at Ellen's plate.

Ellen nodded and quickly took a bite. "It's delicious," she said. And for the first time in months, the food really did taste delicious.

They finished breakfast in silence. Afterward, Pat told Ellen to take a shower while she did the dishes. When Ellen stepped back into the living room, she found the entire room vacuumed and cleaned. She blinked back tears again.

"Why are you doing this?" she asked again.

Pat sat down on the sofa. "I've been here. I know what you're going through."

Of all the people who'd told her that since the divorce, Ellen knew Pat really did know what she was going through.

"Pat, can I ask you a question?" she asked quietly.

"Sure."

"What happened with you?" Ellen held her breath. Had she overstepped her bounds?

Pat looked out the window. "The truth is, John announced to me on his forty-third birthday that he was gay. And he'd been having gay affairs during our entire marriage."

Ellen gasped. "Oh, Pat, I'm so sorry." She tried to imagine Sandy being a man instead of a woman and knew she couldn't have stood the pain.

Pat's eyes shimmered. "It was a long time ago. The hardest was losing my son. He got into drugs right after John left."

Ellen hung her head, feeling ashamed. "I wasn't much help when it happened."

"Oh, no, Ellen, you were fine," Pat assured her.

"No, I wasn't," Ellen contradicted. "I know it now. I've been on the other side for too long, and I see how I turned my back on you just as much as everyone else did." She choked up. "I'm sorry, Pat. We let you down when you needed us the most."

Pat took her hand. "But Jesus never did."

Ellen stiffened and took her hand away. "Then you were lucky."

Pat sat quietly for a few seconds. Finally she spoke. "What happened?"

"They threw me out of that church. I got hate mail. I got verbally abused in Safeway. And it wasn't even my fault. I never want anything to do with the church again!" As her voice rose, she fought to control her anger. "I'm so glad you want to be my friend, but don't think of me as a missionary project. I have no intention of ever going back to the church. If that's the reason you're here, you can leave now."

Silence. *Don't go, don't go, don't go, Ellen found herself thinking. I need someone to talk to. I need someone to be my friend even when they know all the most terrible things about me.*

"That's not why I'm here," Pat said slowly. "I'll be your friend even if you never attend another service."

"Thank you," Ellen choked out.

More silence. "Can I ask you a question?"

"Sure." Ellen shrugged as she answered.

"What about God?"

Ellen turned quickly. "I'm not on great terms with Him either."

Pat looked thoughtful. "I found that He was the only One who got me through the death of my son. I went to counseling, I talked to friends, but people can only take you so far. God is the only One who can go to the deepest points of depression with you."

Ellen glared at her.

"OK, I won't preach," Pat assured her. "And I won't mention it again."

"It wouldn't do any good. All I'd want to read in the Bible would be Job."

Pat smiled. "Then that's where you should start."

Ellen glared at her again.

"Oops, sorry. That's the last sermon. I promise!" Pat

looked toward the kitchen. "You don't have anything to eat in this house. How about we get you some groceries?"

Ellen nodded. "Good idea." She stood slowly and stretched. "I'll go dry my hair."

They drove to the market a half-hour later. Ellen sneaked a glance at Pat as they walked through the automatic doors. Pat shopping on the Sabbath day? She wondered what all the pious church members would think of that.

They purchased several bags of groceries, and Pat helped her unload them into her cupboards. After assuring her she'd call later, Pat left. Ellen opened her "to do" list and wrote a note to make another appointment with the counselor. She felt a little shaky inside, but she knew someone would be there if she needed help. And she also knew someone would notice if she disappeared.

She took the rest of the vodka and the empty pill bottles out to the trash, shutting the lid with a bang. She couldn't believe she'd been so close to taking her own life. It made her shiver as she thought of it.

Back in her living room, Ellen looked at the Bible on the lamp stand. She'd put it there out of habit. The family Bible always went on that stand. She thought of Pat's words. Start with Job. She remembered the story of Job. It never seemed very fair that God would put him through such suffering in order to win a bet with the devil. Job kept all the laws, did everything right, yet God allowed tragedy after tragedy to come on him. Ellen wondered if getting twice as much of everything at the end of the story made up for all the agony Job went through.

She remembered a twelve-year-old Jeff asking her about God.

"Mommy, is God good?"

"Yes, Jeffy. God loves us very, very much."

"Then why does He allow car accidents and cancer and

Auschwitz?" He'd just learned about the Holocaust in school.

"That's the work of the devil, not of God," Ellen told him.

"Who created the devil?"

"God did."

"If God knows everything, why did He create the devil?"

"Because God believes in free will."

"But if God could see that free will would cause car accidents and cancer and Auschwitz, why did He allow it?"

Good question, Ellen thought as she stared at the Bible. She didn't remember how she'd answered him. The questions always nagged at her, though. *Why did God allow evil? How could a loving God use Job to prove a bet?*

There's only one way to find out, she decided and picked up the Bible.

Blowing dust off the cover, she opened the well-worn pages. They brought back memories of family worships with Frank. He always had read from this Bible. She ached inside as she thumbed through the Old Testament chapters. *Why, God? Why?* She found Job and started reading the first chapter. The wager between God and the devil made her angry, and she snapped the Bible shut. But something urged her to keep reading. Opening it again, she read to the passage where Job's friends arrived to cheer him up.

For the first time, she felt Job's pain. She understood. She thought of how she'd ignored Pat's pain years before and felt sick inside.

How many others have I walked away from? she asked herself.

She knew, with sudden shame, that she had blamed other people's misfortunes on them. And even if she had never sent poison pen letters and had never accosted anyone in a grocery store, she was guilty of the same judgmental attitude.

I'm no better than the people I criticized, she admitted.

She'd always been on the "inside" crowd at church. Her father was head elder during her growing-up years. Later, as the pastor's wife, she'd enjoyed being in the center of the church social crowd. Now, on the outside, she could remember the many outsiders she'd ignored—and she hated herself for it.

That's why this happened, she thought. *I'm being punished for criticizing other people. God is punishing me.*

It made sense, but Ellen didn't like the conclusion. What kind of God punished people for simply being ignorant? It didn't seem like a God she could love.

Ellen put the Bible back on the lamp stand and stared at it. Imagining it mocking her, she walked out of the room to get away from it and from her own guilt.

Chapter 12

Thanksgiving. The first one without Frank. Frank and Sandy flew to Hawaii, leaving Jeff with Ellen. Ellen didn't mind. In fact, she felt relieved she didn't have to share Jeff on the holiday. She called her parents and wished them happy Thanksgiving, then tried to make her holiday festive with all the regular trimmings. Jeff tried to pretend as if nothing were missing, but they both knew it was just a façade.

"Have another piece of pumpkin pie," she urged as they reached the end of their meal.

Jeff patted his stomach and groaned. "I can't. I can't even breathe right now, I'm so full!"

Ellen looked at the remains of the meal and tried to sound cheery. "Well, I have lots of leftovers to eat when you go back to school."

Jeff picked at his pie crust. "I wonder what Dad is doing today."

Ellen didn't reply. She looked at her plate and drew a ragged breath. Clenching her teeth, she counted to ten and tried to blink back tears.

"I hope it rains the entire week he's there," Jeff said angrily.

Ellen laughed shortly. "Me too."

She got up slowly and started clearing the dishes off the

table. Jeff stopped her.

"Aren't we going to say what we're thankful for? We always do that when we finish Thanksgiving dinner." His look was pleading.

Ellen sat back down heavily. She didn't want to do anything "like they used to." "You go first," she told him. As she waited for him to start, her mind raced. *What will I say? What can I possibly be thankful for?*

Jeff looked at the candles. "I'm thankful that we're together for Thanksgiving. I'm thankful you can cook so well. I almost starved at school! And I'm thankful I'm sixteen now, and my mom is going to let me get my driver's license this weekend."

Ellen gave him a mock glare. "Dream on."

He looked at her expectantly. "Your turn."

She sighed. "I'm thankful for you and that you're here with me today. I'm thankful for food and shelter . . ." Her voice trailed off. She couldn't think of anything else to be thankful for.

Jeff grinned at her. "So, can I get my license this weekend?"

"We'll see." Ellen stood and cleared the rest of the dishes off the table. "How are things going at school?" she asked.

"Fine. The DMV is open tomorrow."

Ellen raised one eyebrow. "I said I'd think about it. Do you have any idea how much insurance is on a teenage male?"

Jeff put his plate into the dishwasher. "I can take driver's education at school; then the rates will be lower. You could put me on the insurance this summer."

Ellen closed the dishwasher and started it. She sponged off the counters and the table before replying. Jeff watched her, his eyes hopeful.

"All right," Ellen capitulated.

"Yes!" Jeff jumped up and clapped his hands together.

"I'm going to watch the football game, OK?"

Ellen smiled and nodded. Jeff disappeared into the living room, and the TV flicked on. With the kitchen clean and Jeff absorbed in the game, she wondered what she'd do with herself. Read? She felt too restless to read. She walked to her bedroom and picked up her journal. All the pages were still blank. Bob had told her in her counseling session three days before that she should keep a journal. She picked up a pen and started to write.

"Forty-something-isms"

She stopped writing and nibbled on the end of the pen. She had so much she wanted to write about, but her feelings felt stopped up inside. She tried again.

"I don't know where to start. I am feeling a little better since last weekend. I know now that suicide is not for me. But I still feel like I'm in a glass cage where I can see everyone else around me, they can see me, but I can't make them hear me. I feel frozen in pain."

She stopped again. It sounded melodramatic, and Ellen shook her head, disgusted.

"And here I thought my feelings were original," she muttered as she tried writing again.

She propped the bed pillows up behind her and sat on the bed with the journal on her lap. Jeff let out a loud whoop as "his" team made a touchdown.

"It's Thanksgiving Day," she continued. "Jeff is watching TV. I am alone. Like always. Frank and Sandy went to Hawaii. I still hate him. Frank, how could you do this to me? How could you throw me away? God, why am I being punished? Why can't You make everything beautiful again? Why do I hurt so much inside?"

Ellen studied the page. She noticed her pen had dug deeper and deeper into the paper as she had written. "I've forgotten how to write," she whispered as she reread her journal entry.

She started writing again. "I feel worthless . . . a nothing . . . nobody. And I feel guilty. What if it was all my fault? Did I do something horribly bad somewhere in my life? Am I being punished for something now? WHY?! WHY?! WHY?!"

"I'm complaining too much," Ellen muttered. She flipped to the back of the journal and started a list. "Things I am thankful for:"

1. Jeff
2. Food and shelter
3. A job
4. My parents, Katherine, and Pat

She studied the list. Four things. At least it was longer than her Thanksgiving dinner list. She decided to add to the list every day. It made her feel less depressed to look at the words and realize she had four things to be happy for.

The phone rang. Ellen picked it up automatically.

"Hello?"

"Hello, Ellen. Happy Thanksgiving." Bill's voice sounded close enough to touch.

Ellen smiled. "Hi, Bill. Happy Thanksgiving to you too. What a nice surprise! How are you?"

"Doing great. How about you?"

"I've been better," Ellen replied honestly. "But I think things are going to be improving soon."

The TV sound went dead, and Ellen could hear Jeff walk down the hall to her bedroom door.

"I'll be praying for you. If you ever need to talk, just call." Bill's voice sounded warm and concerned.

"Thanks, Bill. And thanks for calling." Ellen felt touched that he'd call on Thanksgiving. *He must remember how hard the first major holiday after divorce can be*, she reasoned.

"While I've got you on the phone, I thought I might mention I'll be up there the second week of December. I wonder if you'd like to get a bite to eat or something." Bill sounded nervous.

"I'd love to see you," Ellen replied warmly. Somehow it was easier to accept an invitation over the phone that it had been in person.

"Well, I won't keep you. Have a great weekend."

"You too. 'Bye."

She hung up and closed her journal. "What is it, Jeff?" she called.

He pushed the door open, his face red and his eyes angry. "Who was that?" he demanded.

Ellen blinked and sat up straight. "A friend."

He leaned against the doorjamb, his hands crammed into his pockets. "Are you going to run off with him?" he asked bluntly.

Ellen gasped. "No, of course not." She got off the bed and tried to hug him. He stood stiffly in her arms.

"Why should I believe you? Dad—" Jeff's voice broke; he started crying harder than Ellen had seen him cry since he didn't make the baseball team in the fifth grade. He kept his face turned from her, his slim shoulders shaking.

Starting to cry too, Ellen hugged him tighter, and he wrapped his arms around her.

"It's not fair," he sobbed. "You guys really had me fooled. I always thought we had the perfect family. Always!"

"So did I," Ellen whispered.

He drew back. "*You* didn't know? *You* couldn't tell?"

Ellen sighed and dropped back down onto the bed. He sat beside her. "I didn't want to know," she said brokenly. "Now, as I look back, there were signs, but at the time, I just didn't see them."

Jeff wiped his eyes. "Adults sure know how to mess up their lives," he muttered.

Ellen nodded. "I hope you realize that what happened between your father and me had nothing to do with you. It was not your fault."

He looked at her strangely. "I know *that*. I've read all the self-help books. Grandma bought me a whole stack of them last summer."

Ellen smiled. Trust Frank's mother to efficiently take charge of the situation. "And, Jeff, I will never leave you. Never." As she said the words, she knew she could never consider suicide again.

"You know, I really hate him sometimes. And I hated you for not making the marriage work." He gave her a quick look. "I'm sorry."

Ellen put an arm around his shoulders. "I understand."

Silence. Jeff gave her a quick smile. "So are you *really* going to let me get my driver's license tomorrow?"

Ellen slapped his arm playfully. "Only if you stop nagging me about it!"

"Deal." He grinned at her.

She stood up. "You want to play a game or watch a video?"

He stretched and stood beside her. "A video sounds good. May I drive there?"

Ellen gave him a warning look. "Jeff, I meant it."

He smiled innocently. "I need the practice. Grandma and Grandpa let me drive in Seattle after I got my permit."

Ellen felt her palms go clammy at the thought of Jeff driving in Seattle traffic. "Where in Seattle?" she asked as she grabbed her coat out of the closet.

"Downtown, on the freeways, anywhere." He squared his shoulders proudly. "I think I can handle a trip to the video store."

Ellen reluctantly handed him the keys. He walked to the van proudly. After they both buckled their seat belts, Jeff backed carefully out of the parking spot and drove to the road. Ellen clutched the sides of her seat and prayed he wouldn't hit anything.

"Jeff, lights! Turn on the lights!"

"Chill, Mom." He flicked them on casually and turned onto the road.

Every new intersection looked fraught with danger. Ellen closed her eyes and tried not to watch, but she couldn't resist peeking.

"Jeff! There's a car coming on your right! Slow down!"

He glared at her. "I saw it."

Let him drive, Ellen told herself. *Let him drive. Just don't watch.* She closed her eyes again.

They arrived safely at the video store. After selecting a video, they started the trip home. Again Ellen clutched the seat, but this time she kept her eyes open and her mouth closed. Jeff looked confident and in control at the wheel of the van. Ellen had no idea when he'd grown up so fast.

Jeff handed her the keys as they entered the condo. She pocketed them safely in her purse.

"You did very well," she praised.

He grinned. "Better than you did watching me."

She shook her head. "You forget I've had quite a few more years of driving experience than you have, and I know the dangers of the road much more than you do."

"Right, Mom." He took the video out of its jacket and put it in the VCR.

Ellen took off her coat and headed for the kitchen. "You want popcorn?" she called.

"Yes!"

She laughed slightly. She still felt too full from Thanksgiving dinner to eat. But Jeff—with his ever-empty stomach—clamored for more food.

She popped the popcorn and took it to the living room. They both sat on the sofa and watched the movie in silence. Ellen couldn't keep her mind on the story. She sneaked looks at Jeff. Already, at sixteen, he was losing that gangly pubescent look. He looked much more mature—almost adult. She felt she was seeing him for the first time. He still had her hair and Frank's eyes, but somehow the familiar combination seemed foreign now.

The movie ended two hours later, and she stood and stretched. Jeff carried the empty popcorn bowl to the kitchen and rinsed it in the sink.

"We should get to the DMV early tomorrow," he called from the kitchen. "Maybe right as it opens. I know how you hate waiting in long lines."

Ellen shook her head and laughed quietly. "We'll get there early," she promised, yawning.

He came out of the kitchen and dropped to the sofa again. "You wanna watch with me?" he asked.

"No. This old lady needs her sleep." She gave him a quick kiss on the cheek, pleased he didn't pull away. "Try and get some sleep tonight yourself, OK? You don't want to be tired for your test tomorrow."

He flicked on the remote control. "Sure, Mom."

She left the living room, knowing he hadn't heard a word she'd said. Closing her bedroom door behind her, she smiled. *You're a great kid, Jeff*, she thought.

She changed quickly and crawled into bed. The sounds of the TV came muffled through the closed door. Every few minutes she could hear Jeff laugh. She rolled over and looked at the lighted face of her clock.

Oh, Jeff, I hope we haven't destroyed your security and trust, she thought. She remembered his tears and felt overwhelmed with guilt. How would Jeff ever learn to trust her again? How would he ever be able to build a successful marriage someday?

God, it's not fair that he has to suffer. He's innocent.

She thought of how she'd almost forgotten about his pain in order to deal with her own. Now, as she felt his pain in addition to her own, she felt guilty as well.

I neglected him. I shipped him off, and I neglected him.

She turned over and stared at the wall. *He's doing OK; he's handling it*, she told herself. But then she remembered his anger over Bill's phone call and cringed. *Maybe I shouldn't have male friends for a while. Maybe it will make him feel more secure if one parent doesn't date right away.*

It's not fair, kept going through her mind.

Finally, after an hour, she fell asleep.

Chapter 13

"Ellen, you are not responsible for Frank's choices. You cannot blame yourself for things he did."

Ellen nodded and blew into a tissue. She sat in Bob's office, trying to pick up what was left of her life. "But I drove him away! I was too judgmental, too harsh . . ."

Bob looked at her kindly. "It was still his decision to go."

Looking at him sadly, Ellen asked, "Then how come I hate myself so much?"

"What do you think?" Bob asked.

"I don't know. Maybe, if it's my fault, then I could have controlled it, and I can still control it."

"So I hear you saying that in taking the blame, you feel you had some control over the outcome."

Ellen thought about that a long moment. "Yes," she announced suddenly. "That's absolutely right. It's not just Frank. I have to have control over every area of my life. If I lose a sale in business, it's my fault. If Jeff is depressed, it's my fault. If I get cut off on the road, for goodness' sake, it's my fault." Ellen grinned humorlessly. "Pathetic, huh?"

"What would happen if you let go? If you stopped beating yourself over everything?" Bob let the question linger.

"I would lose control," Ellen finally whispered.

"Do you have control now? Can you honestly say you can control Frank and your sales and people cutting you off on the road?" he asked quietly.

"No."

He leaned forward in his chair. "Ellen, I am going to tell you something that's absolutely the truth. Are you willing to hear it and accept it?"

She nodded.

"You are not responsible for Frank's leaving. That is Frank's responsibility."

Ellen shook her head. "But I pushed him away. I—"

"Frank made his choice," Bob cut in. "I am not saying you're perfect. None of us are. But it was *his* choice to leave the marriage and *his* choice to get a divorce."

Ellen sat and listened to him. She wanted to believe so badly.

"I want you to try something new this week," Bob continued. "I want you to let go of things you cannot control. Tell yourself you are a good person, and you are not responsible for the actions of Frank or anyone besides yourself. Will you try that?"

Ellen nodded.

"And write about it in your journal." He looked at his appointment book. "Will next week at the same time be good for you?"

Ellen nodded again and automatically made the notation in her own book. "Thank you," she said as she left his office.

She drove through the streets, hardly noticing the bright red-and-green Christmas lights. Her windshield wipers swiped at the ever-present drizzle. Flicking on the radio, she tuned to a station that played only Christmas carols.

As she turned onto the freeway headed west to Park Rapids, she tried to imagine what letting go meant. *Let go. How does a person let go? Does it mean to stop trying?*

She arrived home and ran through the rain to her front door. Slamming it behind her, she shrugged out of her coat and hung it carefully in the closet. The phone rang, and she picked it up a little breathlessly.

"Hello?"

"Hi. This is Pat. How are you?"

Ellen smiled and dropped into a chair. "Great. Thanks. How was your Thanksgiving?"

Pat groaned. "My mother made me crazy. What do you think? I fly clear to L.A. to see her, and she spends the entire time asking me why I haven't visited sooner! Argh!"

Ellen laughed. "Sorry about that."

Pat laughed with her. "Really, I had a nice visit. But I must admit I was glad to fly home. How was your holiday?"

Ellen kicked off her shoes. "Better than I expected. I had Jeff for the weekend, and we had a good time together. He got his driver's license on Friday and was quite proud of himself." She thought, suddenly, of Pat's dead son and felt a rush of guilt. "Pat, how do you let go of something?" she asked, changing the subject quickly.

"Huh?"

"My counselor told me I have to let go of my marriage and my guilt. Do you know what he's talking about?"

Pat laughed. "Yes, but I don't think you'll want to hear my answer."

"Yes I do," Ellen countered.

"I 'let go,' as you call it, by surrendering everything to God. I know that sounds like a cliché, but it's really true. It's accepting that you really have no control over things and that God does."

Silence. "I think I'd like to explore that," Ellen finally said.

Pat's smile was almost audible. "Then begin again with God. It's OK if you're angry and hurt. God understands that; He'll meet you wherever you can meet Him."

"Thanks, Pat," Ellen said softly.

"Call me any time if you want to talk about it."

"Are we still on for lunch tomorrow?" Ellen said hopefully.

"Absolutely. I'll meet you about twelve-thirty. Good night."

"Good night."

Ellen hung up the phone, picked up her shoes, and walked to the bedroom. She changed quickly into a comfortable sweat suit, then fixed herself a light supper. Before settling at the kitchen table to eat, Ellen picked up her Bible and journal. She opened the Bible to Job—it still seemed the most relevant to her life.

After rereading the opening section, she started reading the arguments of the three friends. She realized, as she read, that she'd always skipped over this section and turned to the end, where God rewards Job. Now, for the first time, the middle section seemed interesting.

The three friends made her angry. They voiced the same things she'd heard all her life about the nature of God: God is fair. He rewards good with good and evil with evil. There is a moral order to the universe, and Job broke it. Job must have sinned to deserve such punishment. As she read, Ellen recognized herself in the three friends.

That's me, she realized. *All three of those friends are part of me. I've been using their arguments against other people, and now I've been beating myself up with those same conclusions.*

She thought of the years she'd been taught the three friends' view of God. It had been ingrained in her. But now, suddenly, she knew it had been wrong. She read further.

"Though He slay me, yet will I trust Him."

Job's words for faith brought tears to her eyes, and she blinked them back rapidly. *How could he hang on? How could he keep trusting when everything and everyone he loved had been stripped from him?* She closed the Bible partway through the arguments and opened her journal.

"I don't know what to believe anymore," she wrote. "The past months have stripped so many of my dearly held beliefs from me. How can I believe in the fairness of God? How can I trust a church again? Where do you start when everything has been crushed out of you? 'Though he slay me . . .' God, You've slain me. I have nothing else to hold back. Nothing is safe. Why?"

She stopped writing and stared at the wall for a moment. Her half-eaten food was now cold, and she pushed it out of the way.

"Job's three friends were saying what they thought God had laid down in a covenant years before. I hear their words in the beliefs of Christians everywhere."

She stopped writing and closed the book. Bob's words came to her mind: Let go. Suddenly the absurdity of thinking she had enough power to completely control all aspects of her life struck her, and Ellen started to laugh.

After she rinsed her dishes, Ellen walked to the living room, briefly considered turning on the TV, but decided against it. She sat on the sofa and closed her eyes.

"God, are You here?" she whispered. "I know I haven't spoken to You very nicely for a while, but after starting to read Job, I am beginning to believe You understand. I don't want to pray for things anymore. I just want to learn to let go and leave my problems with You." She laughed softly. "I don't particularly trust You, but I've screwed things up so much that I doubt You can do any worse."

She stopped and opened her eyes. "Maybe I'll just start with my feelings about Frank. If You can handle that, I'll know You'll handle the rest." Ellen figured the problems with Frank couldn't get any worse.

She remembered the words of an old hymn—"Peace, peace, wonderful peace." *Can I have that?* she wondered. *Would it be too much to ask for peace, inside?*

She sat utterly still and waited. For what, she wasn't sure. A sign? An answer? Slowly the knot she'd been carrying inside for months loosened. The pain remained, but the tension disappeared.

"Oh, God, thank You," she whispered.

Is this what peace feels like? Ellen wondered as she prepared for bed. The old restlessness she'd carried around since college had gone. The fear, deep inside—that cold, hard part of her she'd had for as long as she remembered— that was gone too. She slept dreamlessly for the first time since Frank had left.

The feeling of peace remained for the rest of the week. Ellen rose a little earlier each morning, prayed for peace, read a bit more in Job, then tried to honestly leave her problems to God. But the questions still bothered her. *What kind of God would allow this to happen? How could God allow evil in the world at all?*

Bill came into town to visit the second week in December. Ellen, still not sure how much to trust him, agreed to meet him at a restaurant. He stood waiting for her outside the front door.

"Ellen, it's good to see you." He kissed her cheek softly.

Ellen smiled and didn't draw back. "How are you? How was your trip?"

He held the door open for her. They went in and found a seat in the back. "I'm doing great. Better since I'm here with you. My trip was fine." He studied her. "You look beautiful. Happier, somehow."

She blushed slightly. "Thank you. I am happier."

He took her hand and held it gently. His fingers softly caressed the back of her fingers. Ellen closed her eyes and let the sensation of his touch wash over her.

"I've missed you," he said gently.

She opened her eyes. "I've missed you too. Thank you for coming and visiting."

When the waiter walked up, Bill dropped her hand quickly. Ellen missed his fingers on hers. After they ordered, they started discussing everyday things. The moment had passed. Ellen put her hand back out on the table, but Bill made no move to touch her again.

Dinner passed quickly. Bill had her laughing so hard at his stories that people at the other tables turned in curiosity every time they laughed. After paying for the meal, they walked into the dark drizzle together.

"You want to go for a walk?" he asked.

Ellen grinned. "I'd love to."

He took her arm, and they walked slowly, the cold air and the mist making little white puffs of their breath. Under a street lamp, Bill turned and took her face in his hands. He seemed to question her with his eyes. Then, slowly, he gently kissed her.

Ellen had never felt a softer kiss. As it brushed her lips, she closed her eyes, wanting it to continue forever. He then caressed her cheek softly with his hand.

"You're a beautiful woman," he whispered. "And you're a beautiful person inside."

Ellen felt a rush of tears. "Ah . . . thank you."

He turned, and they walked slowly back to their cars. As they reached hers, he spoke again.

"I want to see you again. I knew you were special the first time I met you. I'm not here to waste your time, and I'm not going to waste mine if you're not interested." He stopped and looked at her nervously.

Ellen thought a second. "Bill, I want to see you again. I like you a lot. But I'm not sure that I'm ready for a relationship yet. Can you understand that?"

He nodded.

"If, when I get everything sorted out, you still want to see me, I'd love to see you." She waited breathlessly for his answer.

He touched her face gently. "I'll wait as long as you want," he promised simply. "I've been praying that God would lead me to someone like you. And I'm willing to wait for God's time."

Ellen studied him. "Where do you get that kind of faith?" she asked. "I'm lucky if I can think of God as good."

"It's taken me a lot of time, and I don't always succeed. But God always reminds me to listen to Him." Bill hunched his shoulders against the drizzle.

"You're freezing," Ellen said, unlocking her car door. "I'll call you. I promise."

He kissed her again quickly. "I'll be there. I promise. And I'll be praying for you."

He stood and watched her as she exited the parking lot. Ellen watched him in her rearview mirror until she turned a corner and couldn't see him anymore.

Can I become interested in someone else? she wondered. Right now, she hoped she could survive each day. And she realized she hadn't thought of the future at all. Could she dare trust God with this relationship too?

God, can I trust You? Can I believe You really want the best for me? I never wanted to fall in love again. I'm not sure I want to now. What if he's an ax murderer or a rapist? What if he is like Frank?

She parked the van and let herself into her condo. As she paced the living room, she thought of Bill's gentle kiss. Could he be trusted? She shivered. It had been so long since a man found her attractive.

Just wait, she told herself firmly. *Let go and wait.*

She thought of Jeff and frowned. Would he understand? Would he feel she was deserting him too?

Wait. Just wait.

She wondered if she'd ever learn how to let go.

Chapter 14

As Christmas drew nearer, Ellen plunged deeper into the book of Job. The ancient poetry that had seemed so confusing and boring before now touched her deeply. Job's anger reflected her own. And it made her feel better. To know that God didn't strike Job down for his anger assured Ellen that He still loved her despite her anger.

The anger didn't disappear. It flared up at unexpected times. When she locked herself out of the house in the rain. Or when she had to talk with Frank on the phone. She kept praying for peace, but she didn't always feel it.

"I want Jeff to spend the holiday with me," Frank told her.

They sat across from one another in a restaurant. Frank had called this meeting to talk about Jeff. Ellen thought he looked older, tenser. His hair had thinned dramatically, and the tan he'd acquired in Hawaii only accentuated the fact.

Ellen shredded a napkin in her lap. "Why not let him decide?"

Frank snorted. "He's sixteen years old. What does he know?"

Ellen flushed hotly. "He's almost grown up, Frank. If you were a better father, you'd know that."

He glared at her. "Always have to get a dig in, don't you? That's just like you, Ellen. Always critical."

Ellen blinked back tears. "Maybe he can spend half with you and half with me."

Frank shot her an exasperated look. "You had him all during Thanksgiving."

"It wasn't my idea. You chose to go to Hawaii with *her*."

Frank slammed his hands on the table and stood. "It's impossible. I can't talk with you. I never could. Never mind. We'll split the time between us."

He turned and stalked out of the restaurant. The other patrons turned and stared at Ellen. Flushing hotly, she slunk out to her minivan and drove away.

"I hate you, I hate you, I hate you!" She screamed the words, wishing she had the strength to say them to his face.

Christmas came closer. Frank left a curt message on her answering machine informing her she got Jeff for the first half of the holiday; they got him for the second. Ellen wondered if Jeff would feel like a prize toy they fought over.

She reached the section of Job where God answers Job. It always bothered her that God never answered Job's questions but instead turned the questions back on Job. It didn't seem fair. Ellen had to force herself to keep reading.

"Where were you when I laid the foundations of the earth? Tell Me, if you have understanding."

The questions made her dizzy and a little resentful. Of course Job didn't know. It was an unfair struggle between God and man. And God held all the advantages.

She applied it to her own life. *Where were You, God, when my marriage was falling apart? Where were You when I fell into the maelstrom of depression? Where were You when Your people cruelly rejected me? Answer me, if You know!*

God's questions in Job were her only answer—topping her questions with more questions. She stopped as she reached Job's repentance. Why didn't God give him answers? Why didn't God give her answers?

Jeff arrived home for Christmas break. She decorated

the house with all new Christmas ornaments. She threw out the old ones—afraid of what the memories would bring. The new ones seemed to signify a new beginning.

They had their Christmas on Friday evening. Because Jeff was to spend Christmas Day with Frank, they arbitrarily picked a day for their celebration.

Jeff opened his presents quickly, ripping the wrapping paper like a little boy. Ellen had bought him the usual sweaters and jeans, but this year she also included a key chain with keys to her car and a pair of driving gloves. He ignored the other presents in favor of the keys and the gloves. Donning the smooth leather gloves, he refused to take them off.

"Open your present," he urged.

She unwrapped the paper carefully, enjoying his impatience as she carefully took the tape off.

"Come on, Mom. Just rip the paper!" he urged.

She grinned. "That would take away part of the fun."

A small white box. She opened it carefully and found a silver brooch inside. "Oh, Jeff. It's beautiful!" she gasped.

He smiled proudly. "I thought of you as soon as I saw it. I thought it would look nice on your new business suits."

Ellen smiled. "Thanks. Yes, it will look nice."

He handed her another package. From the size and weight, Ellen knew it was a book. She unwrapped it just as carefully. A leather-bound Bible with her name engraved on it. She looked at Jeff, confused.

"I thought you'd want one of your own. You've always had to use the family Bible." He smiled hopefully at her. "Do you like it? I picked the best one. It has a concordance and everything."

Ellen smiled blankly. "Yes, I love it. But, Jeff, what made you think of this?"

Jeff looked at her seriously. "It's my way of saying I want to go to church with you again."

Ellen drew back and busied herself with the wrapping paper. "I don't know, Jeff. I'm not sure I'm ready."

He continued quietly, "We had a week of prayer at school, and I've given my life to Jesus. Oh, Mom, I wanted to tell you at Thanksgiving, but I didn't know how. Somehow religion has been a sore topic since . . . ah . . . well, you know."

Ellen felt numb. So now she had to hear it from her own son. *You don't give up, do You?* she mentally screamed at God.

"Please, Mom. It would mean so much to me."

She sighed and picked up the Bible. "Out of the mouths of babes," she muttered. "All right, I'll go."

He hugged her. "Good."

That night she looked at the Bible on her night stand and felt sick inside. *God, how can You let this happen? I'm not ready!* She imagined the critical faces, the condemning looks. *I'm not even sure what I think of You yet, let alone church people.*

Sabbath came too early. She silently dressed, fixed Jeff breakfast, and drove to church. He got out of the van and waited patiently for her. Taking a deep breath, she walked into the sanctuary with him. Familiar faces turned and stared at them. Ellen lifted her chin and set her jaw. She stared them back down.

Sliding into a seat, Ellen gripped the edges of her new Bible. As Jeff lustily sang the hymns, Ellen mentally removed herself from the sanctuary. She searched the congregation for Pat before remembering Pat had left town for the holidays.

As soon as the service ended, she rushed outside to the security of the van. Jeff joined her quickly. They said nothing on the way home. As she parked the van, he broke the silence.

"I'm sorry, Mom. I guess I rushed things a little." He

looked bewildered. "It wasn't supposed to work this way."

"Well, it did," Ellen snapped, then softened, seeing his hurt look. "It's OK, Jeff. I know you meant well. But I have many, many things I need to work out with God before I'm ready to go back. Can you understand that?"

He shook his head. "No, but I'll try to."

Ellen climbed out of the van. "There are some things I haven't told you. Many of your father's church members were angry and hostile when your father and I split up. It will take me time to work through that."

He nodded this time. "OK."

She hugged his shoulders. "You're a great kid."

He glared at her.

"Oops, sorry. You're a great young man."

He slugged her playfully. "Knock it off, Mom."

Jeff went to Frank's for the rest of the holiday. On Christmas Day, Ellen slept in, listened to Christmas carols, and tried not to get depressed. Mom called before noon.

"Ellen! Merry Christmas!"

"Hi, Mom. Merry Christmas. Is Dad there?"

"I'm here. Merry Christmas, honey." His familiar voice sounded warm.

"Is Jeff with you today?" Mom asked.

Ellen sighed. "No. We had Christmas last Friday evening, though."

"I don't know why you didn't just get on a plane and come down here," Mom griped. "This independence stuff isn't good for you. You need to be with your family during the holidays!"

Ellen shook her head and tried not to laugh. "Chill, Mom."

"What?"

Ellen laughed. "One of Jeff's phrases. You know, chill out."

"Oh. Well. Whatever."

"I would love to have spent Christmas with you, but the plane fares are terrible in winter. I'll come down this spring after they drop a little, OK?"

"Hmmf."

Ellen smiled. "Merry Christmas. I love you."

"We love you too. Merry Christmas."

As Ellen hung up the phone, she almost wished she had spent the money on a plane ticket. *But I haven't gone home for Christmas for ten years. Why now?* She looked at the phone and debated calling anyone. But, somehow, she knew she had to spend the time alone.

She picked up her new Bible and stared at it. Jeff was right. She'd always used the family Bible. And suddenly she knew she'd always used the family religion. It fit so well, the family religion. She knew the rules, the games, all the right words. But, like the Bible, it had never been truly hers. It had been something she shared with the family that had never been made personal.

She opened the Bible and read the Christmas story. Then, flipping through the elegantly thin pages, she found the last chapter of Job. She started reading at the beginning of the chapter, where Job answers God.

"I know that You can do everything, and that no purpose of Yours can be withheld from You. . . . Therefore I have uttered what I did not understand, Things too wonderful for me, which I did not know. . . ."

Ellen finished the chapter but came back to these words. She put down the Bible and grabbed her journal.

"What does this mean to me?" she wrote. "Do I not understand? Where were you . . . exactly! I don't understand because I can't understand. That's God's answer. God is so far above our intellect that we cannot begin to understand Him or His ways."

She stopped writing, lost in thought. It suddenly seemed

so clear that she couldn't believe she'd missed it so completely before.

"Religions have spent too much time trying to tell people who God is," Ellen wrote. "How arrogant! How can we have even a glimpse of God unless He reveals Himself? How can we presume to explain the greatest power in the universe? We've tried too hard to eliminate the need for faith."

She stopped writing again. *I can't understand because I am not capable of understanding. I have to judge from the small examples in the Bible and from my own life whether God is good. The rest is based on faith.*

"Another thought: Do we as humans have the right to question God? Job seems to indicate we don't have the capabilities to question. And by trying, we lower God to our level of human understanding," Ellen continued telling her journal. "As with everything, it comes to a question of faith. How far will I trust? It's terrifying to trust in something or someone I don't see or understand. How much of my faith is based on what I want to believe rather than what is true? I want to reject this picture because it scares me. I long for an order to the universe that I can understand, but Job tells me I will never understand."

She put her pen down and closed the journal. Outside the living-room window, the rain had turned to snow. Ellen smiled in childlike delight. A white Christmas!

"Have you entered the treasury of snow?"

"We've got it all wrong, don't we, Lord?" Ellen whispered. "I don't understand anything. But somehow that's OK. Help me to trust You on faith, not fact."

She remembered a popular video she'd watched with Jeff. The hero had to take a "walk of faith" off a cliff. He saw no bridge; he had to trust in the legends he'd been taught. Ellen felt that she now hovered at the edge of a cliff, ready to take her walk of faith.

"Lord, I don't know what to believe. Is it OK if I study and watch You for a while?"

Her heart beat faster as she said the words. A thousand questions whirled through her mind. *What about Frank? What about the church people? How can I believe?*

Wait . . . trust . . . hope.

A knock sounded at the door. Ellen looked out the window before opening the door. A group of carolers stood out front, looking cold, but very happy. She opened the door a crack.

"Joy to the world, the Lord has come! Let earth receive her king!"

Ellen shivered against the doorjamb, her eyes shining. After they finished, she gave them money, and they moved to the next door. She sang the words to herself as she shut the door against the cold.

"Joy to the world, the Lord *has* come." She stopped and smiled. *Will I ever be able to understand that also?*

The carolers' voices carried from the next door. "Silent night, holy night." Ellen turned off the house lights and left only the Christmas lights on. And even though the house was empty, Ellen had never felt so surrounded with love.

Chapter 15

January 1. The beginning of a new year. Ellen and Frank's anniversary. While the rest of the world dealt with hangovers, Ellen went down to the river for a long walk.

The cold January air stung her cheeks and made her breath come shorter. She walked fast, trying to keep warm. Trying to forget. *Eighteen years. Today would have been eighteen years.* The thought kept circling through her mind, and she walked faster and faster. Finally, out of breath, she stopped and watched the river.

The winter rains had swollen it, so there was little beach to walk on. The water looked a flat gray that matched the sky. When the drizzle started, Ellen ran back to her van, the wet sand pulling at her feet. Turning on the ignition, she warmed her hands in front of the heater.

The drizzle turned to rain and beat on the van roof as Ellen drove to a restaurant overlooking the river. Only one other person sat in the restaurant, so Ellen found a good table by the window and ordered hot chocolate. Her hands soon warmed, but the coldness inside her remained.

Frank, oh, Frank, I miss you, she thought. *I want to run on the beach with you on the first of January. I want to have hot chocolate with you and laugh and be glad to be alive.*

She remembered their wedding. Small—just family and close friends. After the quiet reception, they drove to Lake

Michigan for their honeymoon. Ellen smiled, remembering everyone's reaction. Lake Michigan? In *January*? You'll get snowed in. But it was a perfect honeymoon. A week in a cabin in the snow. No radio, no TV, no telephone. Just the two of them.

Other anniversaries came back. The five-year trip to the beach. The ten-year trip to Hawaii they had scrimped and saved for. Their first anniversary, when they were so poor they could barely afford a dinner out. They'd dressed up and gone to a diner.

Oh, Frank, I wanted to spend the rest of our anniversaries together. I wanted to celebrate our twenty-fifth, our fiftieth. We've lost so much. We've lost our past because it's too painful to remember. We've lost our future because you forgot. Forgot what? Forgot our vows. Forgot our love for each other.

The years and the memories weighed on Ellen as she sipped her hot chocolate. Outside, on the river, a tugboat chugged slowly by.

Oh, Frank, I don't understand. It's almost been a year since you left, but I still don't understand. What could I have done differently? How could I have changed things? She tried to remember to let go and stop worrying, but she felt helpless against the onslaught of memories crashing in on her. She thought of the previous year's anniversary. Was it only a year ago? They had gone to Timberline Lodge on Mt. Hood. The snow and the rustic lodge reminded Ellen of their honeymoon. She remembered suggesting they come back for their twenty-fifth, and Frank hadn't responded. In retrospect, Ellen knew he was already plotting their divorce.

"Can I get you anything else?"

The waitress's voice startled her. She looked at the empty mug on the table and realized she'd been sitting there for some time.

"No, thank you," Ellen replied absently.

The waitress placed the check on the table and waited discreetly around the corner. Ellen felt annoyed at being pushed out of the restaurant.

"You'd think they wanted the table for something," she muttered as she left a couple bills on the table.

She drove home slowly, not wanting to return to the empty condominium. Even after being there six months, the place didn't feel like home. Ellen always felt she was waiting to get her life going again and wondered how long it would be before she realized this was her life.

The complex was unusually silent. No children ran on the playground, and nobody was out front working on his car. She shut the door behind her and sank to the sofa. Closing her eyes, she listened for something, anything. All was utterly still. Even the neighbor's stereo had quieted.

Everyone's too hungover to do anything, Ellen decided, smiling slightly. Her one bout with alcohol convinced her it wasn't something she ever wanted to drink again.

She looked at the telephone longingly. *Call me, please, Frank. Just call and acknowledge that today still means something to you too. Just admit that seventeen years together wasn't wasted.* The phone stared silently back at her.

She got up and paced the rooms. She grabbed her datebook and started filling all her appointments in her new calendar. She flipped through the months idly. January, February, March, April? Where will I be in April? Or May? Last year I thought I knew what would happen every year of my life. Now I'm not sure what the next day will bring.

A knock sounded at the door. Rising slowly, Ellen patted her hair into place before opening the door. Frank stood in her doorway, shoulders hunched against the chill, his thin hair blowing slightly in the wind.

"May I come in?" He shivered as he spoke.

Ellen moved aside without saying anything and opened the door wider for him. He stood and surveyed the living room, took off his coat, then sat in the wing chair. Ellen felt a stab inside. The wing chair had always been Frank's favorite. She sat on the sofa.

"I don't know why I'm here," he finally said, looking at the walls, the windows, anywhere but at her. "I just got up this morning and went for a drive, and somehow ended up here. I can't explain it."

Ellen didn't say anything. She studied him, thinking the Frank she knew had completely disappeared. The kindness had left his eyes. Now, his eyes looked bitter and his mouth hard. *Have I aged the same way?* Ellen wondered.

"You look good," he said, as if reading her mind.

"Thank you." A short reply. Ellen didn't trust herself to talk much more. Her emotions swirled out of control.

He looked at the room again. "This is a nice place."

"Thank you."

Silence. Awkward silence. Frank stood up and grabbed his coat. "I should go."

Ellen shook her head. "No, it's OK. What did you want to talk with me about?"

He debated a second, then sank back into the chair. "I don't know," he said helplessly. "I don't know what to say or where to start. I guess I just wanted to talk with you, to try to make you understand what happened . . ."

"I'd appreciate that," Ellen whispered.

"Really?"

She nodded.

"I'm not sure what happened—or even when it started. I knew for a long time that something was gone from the ministry and that something was gone from our marriage. Maybe I never truly believed in either one, I don't know. But then there was Sandy, and everything got out of control, and then it was over and—" his voice broke. He bit his knuckles and cried.

Ellen closed her eyes and felt tears slip down her own cheeks.

"Seventeen years . . . almost a lifetime."

Ellen nodded. "I know."

He cleared his throat. Ellen opened her eyes and looked at him.

"Do you still believe in God? Did you ever believe in God?" she asked.

He looked bleak. "I think I did at one time. Now I don't know. I'm not sure God will forgive me." He gave a short laugh. "Isn't that rich? For years I promised people God's forgiveness, and now I don't believe it myself."

"Oh, Frank, God will forgive." The words left her mouth before she had time to think about them. *Do I believe that?* she wondered.

He looked at her for a long moment. "Will you? Will you forgive me, Ellen?"

Ellen drew back and stared at her hands. "I don't know. I want to, but you hurt me so deeply. . . ."

His shoulders slumped. "I understand." Silence. "It's just sometimes I can't think of any reason to get up in the morning. If there's no meaning to the universe or to life, why keep going? Sandy does what she can, but she has no Christian background. She can't understand."

Sliding her feet out of her shoes, Ellen tucked her feet up under her, but said nothing.

"For the last few years I kept trying to find ways to kill myself. I couldn't keep going. Every morning I went to that church and gave and gave and gave. Every *day*! No one ever said thank you. No one ever asked me if I was having a good day. No one ever wanted to listen to my problems. No one ever told me to go away and rest for a while. No, they just kept taking and taking and taking. And one morning, someone walked into my office who wanted to give. And I had no way to resist."

Ellen's tears continued to flow unchecked down her cheeks. "And I kept taking too. Between Jeff and the church, I was never there for you."

"It's not your fault," he said sharply. "Maybe it's both of our faults for not taking time with each other. Maybe we should have set limits on the amount of time we gave to the church. I don't know . . ."

"And we'll never find out," Ellen added quietly. "Why didn't you tell me when I had a chance to do something about it?"

He shrugged. "I don't know. I think by the time I realized what was happening, it was too late."

Ellen nodded. "Yes, I guess it was."

He studied her. "Do you still believe?"

She nodded, then shook her head. "Yes. No. It depends. God and I have had a rough year. I am just now taking baby steps to believe Him again. I have no faith in the church. I hate those people and everything they stand for. They have robbed me of my faith, of my marriage, and of almost everything I once believed in." Her words came out angry and bitter.

Frank looked pained. "I'm so sorry, Ellen."

She bit her lip. "I am too."

The clock chimed, and Frank stood to go. He put on his coat and walked to the door. Ellen followed him. He stopped and kissed her suddenly. She pushed him gently away.

"I think you'd better go," she said firmly, though every part of her begged to let him stay.

He searched her face. "I've missed you."

Ellen opened the door. "Frank, you'd better go."

He gave her one last look before walking out. Ellen shut the door quietly behind him and locked it. Her heart pounded as she walked back to the living room.

"He's another woman's husband now," she told herself firmly. The words tore her up inside.

"What can one time hurt?" another part of her reasoned. "Sandy deserves it."

"No. You are no longer married to him. That's it."

She stood at the window and watched his car drive away. *Come back, oh, please come back. Take me away, and we'll spend a few weeks rediscovering each other.* The car disappeared. Ellen turned from the window and cried.

Can I forgive you? Can I heal? She remembered the text in Romans of how all things work together for good for those who love God. *Is this pain going to work for something good? Will I someday be able to look at Frank without feeling torn apart inside?*

"Oh, God, I don't know if You can be trusted. But I have nowhere else to go. Today is very, very hard for me." She sobbed the words. "I want to follow Frank, to try to work things out. Right now I'd settle for a weekend—or even just a night. How can You promise that something good will come out of this?"

She walked around the house, hugging herself and crying. The stories of the Bible came back to her. Joseph being made ruler after having been sold into slavery and spending years in prison. Moses leading the people of Israel after having spent years in the desert. Esther, Daniel, Ruth. Ruth, who lost her first husband and had to trust in her love for her mother-in-law and the woman's God. All these people trusted God, and He brought something beautiful out of terrible situations.

"God, will You do that for me?"

She thought of the years of her marriage. As she replayed each picture in her mind, she could see all the times she had ignored Frank and his concerns, all the time she was more concerned about her image than the feelings of her family, all the times she withdrew into an icy shell of judgmental condemnation when people refused to live up to her level of perfection.

"All have sinned and fall short of the glory of God."

"Oh, God, forgive me," she whispered brokenly. "I have tried to *be* You rather than worship You."

All her life she'd tried to do everything herself. From trying to create her perfect marriage to trying to create a perfect religion, Ellen realized she'd never faced her own inadequacies. Even after the divorce, she tried to get through it on her own.

"I can't do it on my own anymore, Lord. Please teach me to let go. Teach me to trust You."

She thought of Frank and of the church and gritted her teeth. So much anger and bitterness remained.

"God, it's not fair. I don't want to forgive them. They don't deserve it!"

The answer seemed to come from within herself. "Do I? Do I deserve forgiveness?"

She hung her head. "No. But You'll have to teach me how to forgive them. I can't by myself."

Outside, the light began to fade. The neighbor's stereo started its dull thumping. Ellen's tears subsided, and she knelt in front of the wing chair.

"God, I give everything to You. Give me the faith to trust You. I give You Frank. Please work out what's best with him. Teach me to forgive him. I give You the church. Teach me to forgive it. Most of all, I give You myself. Teach me to forgive myself. Help me to accept the goodness I see in You, and please help me to accept all the vastness I can never understand."

She stopped and rubbed her knees. They were beginning to ache a little. She suddenly remembered long-winded prayers in church when she was a child, and she smiled.

"I'm forty years old, and I still don't have any stamina," she added. "God, I still don't understand why any of this had to happen. I will now stop praying for 'whys' and start praying for acceptance."

She stood up slowly, thinking of God's answer to Job. Instead of seeming condescending, it now seemed the only fair answer God could give Job. If He had tried to tell Job he wouldn't understand, it would have been more difficult for Job to see than when God showed him how little he understood. The wager between God and the devil still didn't seem fair to Ellen. But it was something she knew she had to accept on faith. Her divorce, the treatment by the church—neither seemed fair, but again, she had to accept on faith that God could heal her and use the situation for some good.

She thought again of Ruth. God may not have wanted Ruth's first husband to die, but Ruth was willing to let God work something good out of the tragedy.

Can I? Ellen wondered as she looked out the window. *Will I be able to let God work? Even if it means letting go of my anger?*

The street lights came on outside. They shone mistily through the drizzle. Ellen turned and shut the shades.

Yes, she decided. *Yes.*

Chapter 16

Ellen closed the sale and watched as her new clients signed necessary forms. Outside the window, the April sunshine warmed Park Rapids to an unusually high seventy-eight degrees.

"Thank you," Ellen said with a smile as the clients handed back the forms. "I will get these processed as soon as I get back to the office. Is there anything else I can do for you today?"

"No, thank you," the man replied. "But maybe you can leave a few of your cards. I know a few friends I'd like to recommend you to."

Ellen handed him a few of her business cards. She stood and shook both their hands. "Call me if you have any questions," she said as she walked to the door.

"We will. Thank you."

Ellen stepped into the warm sunshine, her step light in her professional leather pumps. April was turning into a record month. She got back into her van and drove to Katherine's office.

"So, did they sign?" Katherine asked as Ellen walked in the door.

Ellen put the signed copies on Katherine's desk with a grin. "And they want to refer me to friends," she said proudly.

Katherine looked pleased. "It looks like I'll be looking for a new secretary in a few months, huh?"

As Ellen walked to her desk, she wondered what Frank would think. She stopped a second, suddenly realizing she hadn't thought of the divorce for two days.

Am I getting over this? Am I starting to heal? she wondered as she stared at the computer screen.

She thought of the months since New Year's Day. After talking with Frank on their anniversary, her anger started to dissipate. A terrible ache took its place. Over the months of January and February, Ellen had let herself experience all the feelings of rage, anger, despair, and loneliness. By March, she was able to stop blaming Frank and start looking at herself. What she found surprised her.

She saw that she had been just as negligent as Frank in keeping the marriage alive. She saw how she had poured all her energies into the church and Jeff, how she had never had time to listen when Frank really wanted to talk, and, yes, how she had harshly judged Frank, Jeff, and all other people. Admitting her judging hurt the most. Ellen didn't like facing such a harsh picture of herself.

Now, on this warm April day, Ellen flicked through the computer files, barely looking at them. Did this mean it was time to move on? Could she possibly forgive?

She thought of Frank and felt love, hurt, and pity. No anger. The anger seemed washed away by the recognition of her own weaknesses. Stopping work, she picked up the phone and dialed Frank's number. The receptionist put her through to him immediately.

"Hi, this is Ellen," she said as he answered the phone.

"Hi." A wary answer. They hadn't spoken more than necessary since their anniversary.

Ellen closed her eyes and prayed for the courage to continue. "I'd like to have lunch with you sometime this week. We have some things to talk about."

Frank didn't respond for a second. "OK," he finally said.
Ellen took a deep breath. "How about tomorrow?"

"Tomorrow looks fine. You want to meet me somewhere?"

"How about the deli downtown?"

"Fine. I'll see you tomorrow about noon."

"Tomorrow."

Ellen hung up and realized she was shaking. *Can I do this?* she wondered, feeling a bit panicky. *Can I sit across a table from him and be civil?*

She shook her head and concentrated on the computer again. But as she worked through the rest of the afternoon, her thoughts kept returning to Frank and their upcoming lunch. She left work a few minutes early and drove home slowly.

"Oh, God, I'm scared," she said out loud. "I don't want to forgive him. It's so much easier to blame."

But, deep down, Ellen knew she wouldn't ever heal until she could forgive Frank. And, perhaps in forgiving him, forgive herself. Forgive herself for not trying hard enough. Forgive herself for contributing to the breakup. Forgive herself enough to be free to move on.

She slept little and prayed much. After waking every few hours, she finally stopped trying to sleep and got out of bed at five-thirty. She took a shower, ate breakfast, then sat down with her Bible.

Even though she knew all the words by heart, she reread the Lord's Prayer. "Forgive us our debts, as we forgive our debtors."

That text had seemed so easy before. Now it felt like the hardest thing she'd ever been asked to do. Forgive Frank so God could forgive her. Let go of the anger. Let go of the pain. She shut her Bible and looked out the window.

"God, I don't know if I can do this. So much of me still cries to see Frank punished for what he did. Teach me to forgive, not because I want to, but because it is a direct order from You."

She drove to work early and buried herself in paperwork. Every half-hour she checked the clock with a growing sense of fear. She walked to the deli a few minutes early and found a booth, where it would be easier to talk. Frank arrived and smiled warily at her. They got sandwiches, then sat down facing each other.

Frank ate quickly, nervously. He didn't say much, obviously waiting for her to speak. She kept clearing her throat, hoping the words would form magically.

Finally he spoke. "If this is about New Year's, I'm sorry. I don't know what's been the matter with me lately." He looked at his plate. "Everything I thought I wanted I am now questioning."

Ellen felt a rush of pity. "No, Frank, it's not about New Year's. Well, not really."

He waited, not looking at her.

"I . . . um . . . do you remember what you said about needing my forgiveness?" Her voice broke, and she stopped to regain her composure.

He nodded, not lifting his eyes.

"You have it, Frank." As she said the words, a great feeling of weight left her, and she was able to smile. "You have it."

He raised his eyes cautiously. "Do you really mean that? Why, Ellen? I wrecked your life. I ran out on you. Can you really forgive that?"

Her eyes shimmered. "I can't, but God can. He's taught me to forgive you."

Frank looked almost sick. "I used to tell people that. I don't believe it anymore."

Ellen impulsively clutched his hand, then nervously dropped it. "It's true, Frank. God, forgiveness, everything—it's true. He's *real*. Oh, Frank, I wish you could experience it too."

He shook his head cynically. "I ran out on God too, you know. He doesn't want me back, and I'm not sure I want to come back."

Opening her mouth to protest, Ellen quickly closed it. She remembered saying similar words to Pat a few months before. Finally she managed, "All I can say is that for me it's worth it."

He shrugged, his eyes bleak. "Then you're lucky." He looked at the rest of his sandwich, picked it up, and ate it quickly.

Ellen concentrated on her sandwich. As she ate the last few bites, Frank spoke again.

"Thank you, Ellen," he said quietly. He looked at her and touched her face briefly. Then, dropping his hand, he slipped his business expression into place. "It's getting late, and I need to meet with a client," he said, looking at his watch.

Ellen nodded and stood with him. They walked out of the deli together. On the sidewalk, Ellen walked one direction, Frank another. She waited until she'd turned a corner before she let her tears fall.

"God, it hurts," she whispered. "I still love him so much. And I hurt so badly."

She kept her head down and concentrated on not running into other pedestrians.

"Part of me still hopes it can work out. When will I let go?"

She arrived at the office and ducked into the bathroom immediately. Standing in front of the mirror, she tried to stop her tears. Inside, she could feel God's answer.

"Leave it to Me. Let go of Frank. Give Me time."

Ellen nodded helplessly. "But I don't want to let go."

She tried to imagine being free of Frank. Would anyone ever take his place? She hadn't spoken with Bill since before Christmas. Should she call and start dating him again?

Her tears slowly stopped, and she splashed her face with cold water to soothe her swollen eyes. And inside she wondered if she'd ever get over feeling like she'd lost half of herself.

Later that afternoon Katherine walked by her desk and asked if anything was wrong. Ellen smiled wanly.

"I had lunch with Frank today," she admitted.

"What'd he want? Lower child-support payments?" Katherine snorted. Her eyes flashed. Ellen could tell that Katherine was primed for a good gripe session.

"No," Ellen replied slowly. "He wanted my forgiveness."

Katherine threw back her head and laughed. "Right. When you-know-what freezes over."

"I gave it to him."

Katherine stopped laughing abruptly. "What?"

"I gave it to him. I had to forgive him in order to forgive myself. Does that make sense?"

Katherine stared at her. "No. Emphatically no! Ellen, he ran out on you. He doesn't deserve your forgiveness."

"And I don't deserve God's, but He gives it to me anyway," Ellen replied softly.

Katherine drew back slightly. "I don't know about this God stuff. If you believe in a God, how can you accept what happened to you?"

Ellen smiled gently, painfully. "That's the beauty of it. I have to accept that painful things happen and that somehow it makes sense in God's logic—even if it doesn't in mine."

Katherine stared at her again, then gave a mocking smile. "Well, you have more faith than I do, sweetie. The jerk I divorced doesn't deserve an ounce of forgiveness."

Ellen looked at her sadly. "Then how can you ever let go of him?"

"Let go? I've let go!" She glared at Ellen. "I let go the minute my ex walked out that door. I threw his things on the lawn, took his dog to the pound, crashed his car, and washed my hands of him." Her voice broke slightly. "I let go," she said more quietly, her eyes bleak.

Ellen touched her arm gently, and Katherine pulled away. She waved her hands vaguely at the computer screen. "Go type something or file . . ." She turned, walked into her office, and shut the door.

Ellen watched her leave, feeling overwhelmed by sadness. *Katherine, Pat, Frank, me—we're all fighting the same demons. We're all trying our best to deal with the same crushing pain.*

"God, be with her," she whispered. "And with me," she added.

She stayed at work a little late to finish typing some policies. Katherine left without saying anything. Ellen feared she'd overstepped and hoped Katherine wouldn't stay angry. She closed the office at six o'clock and drove home slowly. Tiny colorful sails from the windsurfers dotted the Columbia River. Ellen shivered, thinking that while the air felt unseasonably warm, the water probably was not.

She arrived home feeling tired and emotionally flat. As she changed into comfortable clothes, she tried to put everything out of her mind. But the memories pushed persistently back. She thought of Frank's face, of Katherine's reaction.

When does the "forget" part come in "forgive and forget"? she wondered.

And where does this leave me? Do I have to keep forgiving? Must I forgive the church as well? The thought galled her. Every time she imagined walking through the front doors of the church, she felt nauseated. In her mind, Frank had reasons for doing what he did; the church did not. In a time when she needed love and support more than ever before, the church members ignored her.

"I can't, Lord. I just can't. Isn't forgiving Frank enough?"

No answer. Ellen knew inside what the answer should be, but she didn't want to face it.

She grabbed a quick supper and sat down to open her mail. In the middle of all the junk mail and bills, a personal envelope caught her attention. Postmark Eugene. She tore it open eagerly.

Dear Ellen:

I know I said I'd wait for you to contact me, but I couldn't wait any longer. How are you? I miss you. I've been praying for you every day. If you've felt a surge of power every morning about eight, it's my prayer.

Ellen smiled and bit her lip. As she thought of it, she guessed she did feel a little more optimistic in the morning. She kept reading.

I know I don't want to rush you, but could you give me a hint? Maybe just a postcard or a letter? I promise I won't push. But every day I wake up and think about your beautiful dark eyes and hair, and I pray God will let me see you again.

All right, I've been too pushy and maudlin for one letter. Call me any time, day or night. Or write!

Sincerely? Friends? I don't know how to sign this.

Bill.

Ellen laughed softly and reread the letter. Should I call him? She put down the letter and dialed her mother's number.

"Mom, it's Ellen!"

"Who else is going to call me Mom?"

Ellen laughed. "May I ask some advice?"

"Sure." Her mother's voice sounded surprised.

"There's a Christian man I met last August. He wants to date me. But I don't know if it's too early or if he's the right one . . ." her voice trailed off.

Mom laughed. "You don't need to marry him."

Ellen let out a breath. "No, I guess you're right. It's just dating, not marriage."

A silence, then, "Oh, honey, I never thought you'd be dating again."

Ellen choked up. "Me neither."

A few sniffles. "So, how do *you* feel about this man?"

"I like him," Ellen admitted. "He has a talent for saying the wrong thing at the wrong time, he has too much enthusiasm and not enough tact, and he's one of the most sensitive men I've ever met."

"He sounds wonderful," Mom said quietly.

Ellen knew what she was thinking. *Can you trust him? Will he be another Frank?* "I guess I'll just have to trust him and give this dating thing a try," she said aloud.

"I just wish I could meet him first," Mom grumbled. "You won't let him into your condo or anything, will you? You never know these days. Why, down here in Florida, a woman was murdered right in her own bed by some guy—"

"Mom!" Ellen cut her off with a laugh. "That's enough. I already have to deal with my own fears!"

"Well, I just want you to be careful."

"Thanks, Mom. I love you. Give my love to Daddy."

"I love you too. I'll be praying for you."

Ellen hung up and looked at Bill's letter again. He'd written his phone number in bold black letters across the top and the bottom of the page. She looked at the phone, her stomach churning.

"Oh, God, is this the right thing?" she whispered.

She decided not to call, then decided to call. Picking up the letter again, Ellen admitted that she missed Bill. She took a deep breath and picked up the receiver.

It's just a date, right? she reminded herself.

Looking at the letter again, she dialed Bill's number.

Chapter 17

Bill came up to visit the next weekend. And the weekend after that. Ellen kept things casual between them, afraid to trust too soon. Bill accepted that and seemed to enjoy just spending time with her.

"Whenever you're ready for something more serious, let me know," he told her. "I won't push."

And he didn't. He faithfully called, wrote, and visited without asking for more than her companionship and an occasional chaste kiss. Ellen stopped worrying about the future and whether Bill was the "right" man for her. Instead, she prayed about it, then just took each of Bill's visits as they came.

Jeff came home from boarding school at the beginning of June and reacted suspiciously to her growing friendship with Bill. When Ellen introduced the two of them, she could see Jeff analyzing Bill carefully.

"Good to meet you, Jeff. Your mother's told me much about you." Bill heartily shook Jeff's hand and didn't seem to sense Jeff's reserve.

"Nice to meet you, sir," Jeff mumbled politely.

Ellen watched the exchange nervously. After a few minutes of strained conversation about what school Jeff went to and what football team he liked best, Jeff excused himself and went for a walk. Ellen watched him leave, unconsciously biting her lip with tension.

"It's OK, Ellen," Bill said softly.

Ellen studied her hands. "It's just so hard for him . . ."

Bill smiled and took one of her hands. "Hey, I'm willing to wait till he sees what a great guy I am. It worked with you."

Reluctantly, Ellen admitted, "I guess you're right."

That evening Ellen sat down with Jeff in the living room. He didn't look up from his book.

She cleared her throat. "Well?" she asked tentatively.

He looked at her briefly, then went back to his book. "Well what?"

"What do you think of him?"

Jeff sighed and closed the book. "He's nice enough, I guess."

Ellen nodded. "He really likes you, you know."

Jeff looked annoyed. "So? Big deal."

Ellen tried to smile at him. "Hey, buddy, it's OK. I'm just dating him."

He relaxed a little. "I know. But it's still hard to watch."

"It's hard to do," Ellen admitted.

They gave each other a look of silent understanding, and Ellen again marveled at how mature he'd become. She'd almost stopped thinking of him as a kid. And in brief snatches she could clearly see the adult he'd become.

June passed quickly. Jeff worked a summer job in a fast-food restaurant, and Ellen cut back on her evening sales work to spend time with him. He spent every other week with Frank and Sandy. But on the weekends Jeff spent with her, Ellen went to church with him.

The church attendance surprised him the most. Ellen forced herself to attend and refused to let herself walk out—even during sermons she didn't agree with. She looked at the church people differently now. While she didn't trust them, she could see how she had been guilty of the same judgmental behavior when she'd been on the inside.

On the inside. Ellen thought of her life as a "before and after." Before the divorce—on the inside of the church and of society. After the divorce—on the outside. And no matter how friendly people were toward her, she couldn't feel a part of the church community the way she used to.

"Pat, I'll never belong here," she complained after church one day. "It doesn't feel the same. It doesn't feel like a nice, safe family anymore." She bit her lip. "I used to know what I believed about everything. Now I have to start from the beginning and relearn from a new perspective."

Pat nodded. "I am still going through the same thing." She paused. "Maybe it's good that you're wary."

Ellen raised her eyebrows questioningly.

"You've been hurt. God needs time to heal you."

"I've lost my innocence."

Pat responded gently, "And as a result, you can start growing."

Ellen thought about Pat's words for weeks afterward. *I can start growing. Maybe when I was "inside," I couldn't grow in Christ because I thought I had all the answers. Now I have to be open to God. I have to let Him redefine my beliefs.*

She hoped knowing this would make her feel more comfortable in church each week. Sometimes it did. Other times she had to spend the day at the river instead of going to church. Some days anger and bitterness overwhelmed her, and she swore never to return to church. But each time, God slowly turned her around.

"I can't keep my religion going on my own," Ellen wrote in her journal. "Worshiping by myself—throwing off the necessity of a church family—is just as much narcissism as my old self-constructed religion. If only I could have the church without all the people."

The summer wore on. The weather climbed to its usual

scorching temperatures, and Jeff spent most of his free time windsurfing. Ellen concentrated on selling as many policies as she could. She and Katherine planned an October opening for her Park Rapids office.

"You sure I'll be ready by October?" Ellen worried.

Katherine looked exasperated. "Trust me!"

"I'm trying. But living on straight commission scares me!"

The weeks slid by. As she got to know more church members, she started feeling like part of the family again. She no longer cringed when people walked up to talk to her. She and Jeff found themselves invited out to lunch after church and included in church socials. And when Bill visited, they included him also. Ellen was amused to see the older women in the congregation working to push the relationship forward.

August arrived with hundred-degree weather and a church scandal. Ellen heard about it as she arrived for the morning service. People's whispers floated around her, and she heard snatches of the story as she entered the building.

". . . heard he arrived home drunk again . . . how could he do that to Gloria and the children . . ."

". . . and this isn't the first time. I think it's time we sent a delegation of elders to speak with him . . ."

". . . probably a ninety-day rehabilitation . . . it's not his first, you know . . . I wonder what the youth will think? Jake being youth leader and all . . ."

Ellen leaned over the pew to the people in front of her. "What happened?" she asked.

The woman puffed up with the importance of her knowledge. "I heard," she said emphatically, "that Jake Ballston fell off the wagon again, if you know what I mean." She looked the perfect blend of outraged shock and malicious glee.

Ellen gasped. "Jake? He's the youth leader, right?"

The woman nodded. "And that's not all. Apparently his son found him passed out on the lawn. Can you imagine? A six-year-old boy finding his father dead drunk on his own lawn!" The woman's nostrils flared indignantly. "Some people should learn to control themselves!"

Ellen felt her own anger rising. "Absolutely," she agreed. In front, the song leader started directing the hymns. Brimming with righteous indignation, Ellen opened the hymn book to join in the singing. She wanted to march over to Jake's house and tell him what she thought. Imagine, knowing you had a problem and not doing anything about it. How could anyone drink when he had young, impressionable children at home? She ached inside for the young children and for Gloria, the man's wife.

She heard little of the service. After driving home, she got her journal and walked to the river. She found a spot on the beach where she could watch the windsurfers. She didn't write for a few minutes. Every time she thought of Jake, she gritted her teeth.

"People like that shouldn't be allowed to come into our churches and corrupt our youth," she wrote. "He should go away, get control of his problems, then possibly come back, but not to a position of leadership."

She stopped writing and reread her own words. Suddenly realizing what she had written, Ellen began shaking. She dropped the journal on the sand, tears slowly starting.

"Oh, Lord, forgive me," she whispered.

She looked at the words again and felt sick. They closely paralleled the ideas in the hate letter she'd received a year before. What she lacked in words, she'd made up in sentiment.

And I was so proud of being nonjudgmental, she admitted.

Her anger at Jake fled. Suddenly she felt terribly sorry for him. She wondered if he would receive hate letters. She wondered if Gloria would be ostracized from the church as well. She wondered what problems Jake faced that caused him to turn to alcohol for relief. And she wondered if it was too late to try and reach them.

Standing up, she grabbed her journal and brushed sand off herself. She walked briskly back to her condo, each step echoing her thoughts. *I must show them someone still loves them. I must give them another picture of Christians.*

At home she found some writing paper. Picking up a pen, she wrote the letter she wished someone had written her more than a year ago when Frank left.

Dear Gloria and Jake:

You don't know me well, but I am a new member of the Park Rapids Church. As it was mentioned in church that you are being prayed for, I took the liberty of writing.

We love you at the Park Rapids Church. You are part of our family, and we want you to feel acceptance and love here. Please know I will always be a friend if you need one. Call any time, day or night, just to talk, for baby-sitting, or maybe just to grab lunch together.

Ellen signed her name to the letter and addressed the envelope quickly. She dropped it in the mailbox before she could change her mind.

Is this my new role now? she wondered. *Will God use me to help other people because I have been on the outside? Will I ever stop judging people enough to see their hurting?* Ellen asked herself.

She thought of the year she spent recovering from the humiliation of her divorce, her bitterness with the church, and her anger with God. She knew no one could have totally removed the pain, but having a friend to talk to would have eased much of the loneliness and isolation.

Will I be that person to others? she asked herself. *Am I brave enough to be that person?*

She thought of Pat finding her drunk and suicidally depressed. She thought of how Pat could step outside the carefully defined beliefs and rules of the church and really listen to her.

"God, please teach me to stop judging long enough to really listen," she whispered.

Somehow she knew this was a prayer God would answer.

Chapter 18

Ellen stood in church, Jeff on one side, Bill on the other. They shared a hymnbook between the three of them. "Seeking the Lost"—an old favorite hymn of Ellen's. Jeff's melodious tenor clashed with Bill's low growl. She stopped singing on the second verse and just listened.

> Seeking the lost—and pointing to Jesus
> Souls that are weak and hearts that are sore,
> Leading them forth in ways of salvation,
> Showing the path to life evermore.

"Ways of salvation." Ellen wasn't sure she knew the ways of salvation. But she did know that holding a hand through a dark night, grocery shopping for someone in need, just being there for someone who needed to talk—that had to be part of it.

She thought of the previous year and a half. The divorce still hurt. She ached for Frank with a dull hurt that never went away. And no one would ever take his place. She still got angry when people tried to say it was "God's will" or that it was "for the best" that she and Frank got divorced. She doubted inside that it would ever feel like it was for the best. But she trusted God enough to believe He would bring something good out of the tragedy.

She sneaked a look at Jeff. His face glowed as he sang the words of the hymn. Ellen felt so proud of him. She remembered his earnest face as he told her about his conversion. She thought of the Bible he'd given her and smiled.

"Thank You, Lord," she whispered.

Bill sang heartily, if off-tune, on her right side. Would things work out with him? Would they ever have a serious relationship? Ellen didn't know. But right now, right here, it felt good to be standing next to him.

She looked at the other members of the church. Some of them she loved and was starting to trust; others she prayed she'd learn to love and accept. But instead of seeing them as perfect, the way she had before her divorce, or monsters, the way she had immediately after, she saw them as people. People who hurt and cried. People who laughed and celebrated. People who needed her as much as she needed them. Ellen smiled and joined the congregation on the last verse.

> Thus I would go on missions of mercy,
> Following Christ from day unto day,
> Cheering the faint and raising the fallen,
> Pointing the lost to Jesus, the Way.

Would the pain ever totally go away? No. Would she ever totally trust the church again? No. But now Ellen knew the only person she could ever totally trust was Jesus. And somehow that felt right.

The song ended, Bill put the hymnal back in the rack, and they sat down together. As Ellen looked at Bill, Jeff, and the earnest people sitting around her, she felt overwhelmed with blessing.

"Thank You, Lord," she silently prayed. "I've been so blessed."

And for the first time since her divorce, she knew it was true.